THE ZULU

THE ZULUS OF NEW YORK

Zakes Mda

UMUZI

Published in 2019 by Umuzi,
an imprint of Penguin Random House South Africa (Pty) Ltd
Company Reg No 1953/000441/07
The Estuaries No 4, Oxbow Crescent, Century Avenue,
Century City, 7441, South Africa
PO Box 1144, Cape Town, 8000, South Africa
umuzi@penguinrandomhouse.co.za
www.penguinrandomhouse.co.za

First edition, first printing 2019
9 8 7 6 5 4 3 2 1

ISBN 978-1-4152-1015-4 (Print)
ISBN 978-1-4152-1039-0 (ePub)

Cover design by Gretchen van der Byl
Text design by Chérie Collins
Set in 12 on 17 pt Adobe Caslon Pro

Printed and bound by Novus Print, a Novus Holdings company.
Penguin Random House is committed to a sustainable future
for our business, our readers and our planet. This book is made
from Forest Stewardship Council® certified paper.

I dedicate this novel to my dear friend Robert 'Bob' Edgar, a Howard University Professor Emeritus, whose work, co-written with Robert Trent Vinson, 'Zulus Abroad: Cultural Representations and Educational Experiences of Zulus in America, 1880–1945' (published in the *Journal of Southern African Studies*, Volume 33, Number 1, March 2007), sparked my interest in the subject. I am grateful for his encouragement in writing this novel.

I am also grateful to Shane Peacock for his work 'Africa Meets The Great Farini' in *Africans on Stage: Studies in Ethnological Show Business*, edited by Bernth Lindfors (Indiana University Press, Bloomington 1999); to Paulina Dlamini for *Servant of Two Kings*, compiled by H. Filter and translated by S. Bourquin (University of Natal Press, Pietermaritzburg 1986); to Francis Mading Deng for *The Dinka of Sudan* (Waveland Press, Prospect Heights 1984); and to Godfrey Lienhardt for *Divinity and Experience: The Religion of the Dinka* (Clarendon Press, Oxford 1961). Thanks to Elelwani Netshifhire for her contribution in shaping this story.

The novel was completed and fine-tuned during my sojourn as Artist in Residence at the Stellenbosch Institute for Advanced Study (STIAS). I am grateful to STIAS for the generous support.

I

New York City – November 1885
The Wild Zulu

The Wild Zulu. That's what the banner says. Crowds line up at Longacre Square to pay their admission fee into an arena encompassed by bales of hay. Some are already sitting on the bales that are randomly placed on the ground, while others are massing in front of an iron cage.

The Wild Zulu sits in the cage and is resplendent in faux tiger skins and ostrich feathers. He is a giant of a man, bigger than any man Em-Pee has seen. He roars and the spectators gasp in anticipation. A Mulatto urchin outside the cage accompanies the rumble with a conga drum and a tambourine.

The spectators are a motley assemblage of dandies who must have strayed from the saloons, peep shows and gambling dens of the nearby Tenderloin, and workmen in overalls on a lunch break from the carriage factories, tanneries, saddleries, harness shops and horse dealerships that pervade the vicinity. Some of the gentlemen, probably out-of-towners, are accompanied by ladies in their finery.

7

The drummer boy performs a grotesque jig as he beats the conga. He is, however, subdued so as not to steal attention from the main attraction in the cage.

The Wild Zulu's pecs ripple and his bloodshot eyes protrude and roll out of sync. The impresario, a pudgy White man in friendly muttonchops and a shiny stovepipe hat, struts in front of the cage. He is no longer the genial Davis that Em-Pee and Slaw met a week ago when he arranged for Em-Pee to come check out the show. He is all business and does not even cast a glance in Em-Pee's direction. He cracks a whip; The Wild Zulu roars even louder. The dudes cheer and their ladies quiver, holding tightly on their beaux's arms. The workmen, clustering mostly at the rear of the makeshift arena in deference to the upper-crust folks, heckle as they chomp from their lunch boxes, 'Come on, let's see some action! We ain't got all day!'

'Ladies and gentlemen, boys and girls, dudes, dudines and dudesses, now for the most exciting part,' says the impresario, playing to the ladies. He turns to those who are so close to the cage they are almost touching the bars. 'Be careful,' he warns them ominously. 'Stay clear of the cage lest The Wild Zulu reach for your limb between the bars and tear it to pieces with his teeth. He's very hungry, and like all the race of his tribe he is partial to human flesh. He hasn't had a morsel for two days.'

A kindly lady throws a banana into the cage. The Wild Zulu roars and kicks it out.

'What a waste of luxury fruit,' exclaims a man, reaching for the banana.

Davis, on the other hand, is livid.

'Don't feed The Wild Zulu!' he yells. 'What makes you think he eats bananas like a monkey? The Wild Zulu ain't no monkey. He's deadly. He's not called The Wild Zulu for nothing. In their natural habitat baby Zulus suckle from she-wolves. They wrestle with grizzly bears as a rite of passage when they are teenagers. Stand back, stand back! You don't want to provoke The Wild Zulu or he'll eat you for breakfast.'

The crowd is on edge as it gives way for a Black man in dungarees pushing a wooden wheelbarrow laden with raw meat and a live cockerel, its legs tied together with twine. The bird flaps its wings frantically as the Black man transfers the wheelbarrow and its contents to Davis. The impresario carefully unlocks the cage, throws in the chicken and the meat and shuts the door quickly before The Wild Zulu can pounce on him. The spectators scream and shriek as The Wild Zulu dives for the chicken. He rips it to pieces with his bare hands and teeth and begins to eat it alive. Blood splashes all over the cage as he chews voraciously on its innards. He reaches for a chunk of meat and takes a bite from it and then from the chicken, chewing it with feathers and all. The spectators are frenzied, as if thrilling currents are jolting their way through their bodies.

Em-Pee can no longer stomach it. He walks away. But only a few steps behind the cage. His mouth fills with saliva and he spits it out in a jet.

He lingers for some time near the baled-hay barrier but does not exit, fearing that the entrance-keepers may not let him in again. Davis will not be there to explain to them that he is his special guest. Some bouncers are busy shooing away the opportunists who are trying to view the performance from outside over the barrier.

He stands on a bale and watches a barker walking up and down the sidewalk reciting superlatives about the ferociousness and savage prowess of The Wild Zulu and inviting passers-by to come and see the spectacle for themselves. The barker strays into the street, still touting the merits of the show among stagecoaches and hansoms whose drivers are yelling and shaking their fists at what has developed into a traffic jam. For Em-Pee they are more entertaining than The Wild Zulu. He watches for a while and wonders if Slaw will make it on time.

His stomach has calmed down. He must force himself to watch the whole performance. He has no choice. Slaw will demand a full report. Every detail from the beginning to the end. So he drags his feet back. People give way until he is at his original spot in front of the cage. Curious eyes follow him. Perhaps they think he's connected to the show somehow; maybe he's a labourer in the employ of the impresario. He is the only Black man in this audience of New York's gentry and sundry aspirants to status.

Once such spectacles were the preserve of the lower rungs of society while the crème de la crème took refuge in the private boxes of the Academy of Music Opera House and, most recently, the Metropolitan Opera House – opened only a month ago by old money that feels squeezed out of the Academy by the nouveaux riches. But these days not only do these circuses attract the vulgus and the pretenders to wealth and class, but some of the important names of the city have been spotted enjoying the gore, especially when they are staged at such venues as Madison Square Garden. Even the denizens of Broadway theatre establishments can be sighted occasionally indulging in them. All thanks to the most supreme impresario of all time, the one and only, The Great Farini, who has popularised such shows and has turned them into respectable entertainment. Many a member of the New York intelligentsia becomes a regular at these spectacles of primitive races under the pretext of being an exponent of popular anthropology or an aficionado of Charles Darwin's postulations.

The Wild Zulu is now performing a crude dance, groaning and simulating sexual activity. Under the array of skins hanging from his waist to mid-thigh Em-Pee can see what purports to be his mammoth truncheon bobbing up and down. The ladies blush and giggle shyly and the gentlemen are mostly stone-faced.

Some of the workmen begin to stream out, not as a protest against the performance, for they are laughing and egging The Wild Zulu on. It must be time to return to their workstations.

'The Zulus are a very virile race of people,' announces the impresario, winking at the audience.

Em-Pee grimaces.

The drummer boy beats his conga faster, both with his hand and with the tambourine. The Wild Zulu becomes even more frenzied in his dance. He is now focusing his gaze on one particular lady in the audience and is beckoning her, pointing at his ungovernable truncheon. He is ogling her with bedroom eyes while dazzling her with what he imagines is a come-hither smile but looks like a menacing grin instead. The lady cringes into the protective arms of her beau, her face contorted in disgust. The Wild Zulu is persistent in targeting the hapless lady with his rude gestures.

Her beau cannot take it any longer. He hurls some choice invective at both The Wild Zulu and Davis. All hell breaks loose as the spectators heckle and curse while throwing all sorts of missiles at the cage, mostly chicken bones, bits of food and peanuts on which they were snacking. The remaining workmen are armed with even more potent weapons – rotten eggs and fruit, which they hurl into the cage. Davis raises his hands, pleading with the crowd to stop. But The Wild Zulu continues dancing while either ducking the missiles or catching some and flinging them back at the crowd.

Em-Pee takes this as his cue to leave. He negotiates his way through the mayhem until he reaches the entrance. 'You'll be missing the best part,' says the entrance-keeper. 'You'll have to pay again if you come back.'

'He didn't pay the first time,' says another. 'The boss said to let him in.'

'How come they let you in? You don't see no one like you here.'

'Ask your boss,' says Em-Pee as he pushes his way out.

He hastens his gait as he passes vendors who seem to be competing as to who can yell the loudest for his custom. 'Fresh roasted peanuts!'

He stands on the sidewalk and watches the traffic, now less chock-a-block than before. A small group of boisterous smithies and wheelwrights from a nearby carriage factory tease him about his muscular arms, expressing their nostalgia for the good old days when he would have been pulling a coach like a mule instead of loitering in the street.

A hansom comes to an abrupt stop near him, and Slaw alights. He could be mistaken for an Old West dandy, with a riding whip in one hand, which makes Em-Pee chuckle because Slaw is neither a horse rider nor a horse owner. The whip is mere accoutrement.

'How did it go?' Slaw asks.

Em-Pee leads him down the street to the horsecar station. They have only a while to wait. As soon as the horsecar stops, they both climb on the back platform.

'There is room for you inside, sir,' says the conductor, beckoning Slaw.

'I'll be good,' says Slaw. 'I need to conversate with my man here.'

They can hold their conversation only on the exterior platform either at the back or the front because Em-Pee is not usually permitted into the horsecars and omnibuses except at the occasional whim of the conductor – provided the White passengers don't object. Otherwise he must wait for the Coloured cars, which are often rickety and dilapidated and are few and far between. He hates it when Slaw pleads with the conductor on his behalf, pretending that Em-Pee is his domestic help. But when the weather is inclement, he has no choice but to keep up the charade.

They are silent for a while, listening to the clip-clop of the shod hooves and the grinding wheels on the metal rails.

'There is nothing we can learn from those folks,' Em-Pee says finally.

'Those folks mint dough. Lots of it. And you say

there's nothing we can learn from them?' asks Slaw.

'They don't make it the right way,' says Em-Pee.

He tells Slaw about the performance of The Wild Zulu and how offensive it was. Slaw shakes his head and laughs.

'That's exactly what people want to see,' he says. 'They come in their hundreds to be offended.'

'But they threw stuff at Davis and his huge Zulu guy.'

'Where do you think they got the stuff from?' asks Slaw. 'They bring it with them specially for that ... rotten tomatoes and rotten eggs. You know why? 'Cause they expect to be offended. They look forward to it. Listen to me, Em-Pee, Davis is smart and ambitious. He aims to be the next Farini.'

'No one can be like The Great Farini,' says Em-Pee.

'Davis don't work blindly. He analyses stuff like a scientist. Like The Great Farini.'

Slaw explains that successful impresarios operate on two pleasure principles, either to titillate or to offend. He learned that from The Great Farini himself. They often choose one or the other. The genius of Davis has combined the two principles in one show. At one moment he titillates, at another he offends.

'I didn't see nothing titillating in The Wild Zulu,' says Em-Pee.

'Because you decided from the outset that you were disgusted and therefore didn't pay any attention. And I

sent you there to pay attention. From what you out-
lined to me, he began by titillating the crowds. Folks
get titillated like hell when they watch a savage tear
a live chicken with his bare hands and teeth. All that
blood gives them orgasms. Then he offends them with
his crude sexual dance. You saw their crazed eyes. Sheer
genius.'

They get off at Worth Street and walk towards Five
Points.

'I don't like the idea of performing out there in the
open,' says Em-Pee.

'Davis makes more money with outdoor performances. He doesn't have to pay high venue fees. And he can
move his show to any place in the city where folks are
concentrated.'

They are only a few yards into Five Points when a
stench assails them. Soon they see its source – the car-
cass of a horse in the street. It's been there for two days
already and no one has bothered to remove it. It happens
like that in these rookeries, the worst in New York. A
black cloud of flies is hovering over the feast.

The men skirt around a pool of dirty water and a herd
of pigs grunting their way to a pile of street-side gar-
bage.

'I think we should just continue with our Friendly
Zulus,' says Em-Pee, as they reach their Mulberry Bend
tenement.

'You say the damnedest things, Em-Pee, you know that?' says Slaw. 'Who the hell wants to see friendly Zulus in America?'

2

kwaZulu – December 1878
Ozithulele The Silent One

His Zulu colleagues call him Mpi, which has become Em-Pee to the English-speakers. It is less punishing to the inexperienced tongue than Mpiyezintombi – Battle of the Maidens – so named because his father thought he was so handsome that women were going to fight over him.

When they are drinking beer all by themselves, without the White troupe members, the Zulus recite their clan praises. He takes pride in his name, Mpiyezintombi Mkhize, begotten by Khabazela kaMavovo, descendant of Sibiside, he who led the abaMbo people from the blue lakes of central Africa, many centuries ago, to the area that later became known as kwaZulu, where they were incorporated into the amaZulu nation through King Shaka's spear in the nineteenth century.

When he recites his praises, his colleagues ululate like women and it takes Mpi back to the old country where he used to carouse with the young women of King Cetshwayo kaMpande's isigodlo – the very behaviour that brought about his downfall and his flight from the kingdom.

His escape had been unpremeditated. He carried nothing but his spear and shield when he set off from Ondini in the deep of the night. Occasionally he listened on the ground to the sounds of the night, hoping that none of them would be from the heavy gait of amabutho, his warrior colleagues, sent by King Cetshwayo to capture him.

When the December sun rose and scorched his back, he took circuitous routes through the bushes. But soon he would be out in the open veld and the humid heat would do its business on his skin. Occasionally he stood on a hillock and looked back. There was no sign of anyone chasing him and he was relieved. But he would not feel safe until he reached uKhahlamba Mountains and crossed rivers into the land of King Letsie, where he would seek asylum.

Letsie's father, Moshoeshoe, had established a reputation for wisdom and generosity. From the exiles of many nations, he had formed his formidable Basotho nation. Perhaps his son had inherited similar traits and would give succour to Mpiyezintombi, son of Mkhize, who was running away from the wrath of Ozithulele, the Silent One, as Cetshwayo was called.

Mpiyezintombi cursed his foolish lust as if it was something out there acting independently of him. It was fine when he was just playing the fool with the young women of the King's isigodlo, clowning about, making them laugh with his antics and gourmandising the delicacies left over from the King's bowls that the young women furtively placed at his door. The mistake happened when he fell in love with one of them – the plump, yellow-coloured Nomalanga. It was an illicit desire, for she belonged to the isigodlo – the royal household comprising the residences of the King's wives and children, and also the private enclosures of the girls presented to him by various vassals as tribute, or selected by him from distinguished families among his subjects to serve him, purportedly as his adopted daughters. Nomalanga was one such girl.

As he traversed hills and crossed rivers, Mpiyezintombi regretted that he had not stolen one of John Dunn's horses. His flight would have been more comfortable, and he would be far by now. Jantoni, as his fellow amaZulu called John Dunn, wouldn't have missed one measly horse when he boasted a harras of thoroughbreds. Even if he eventually discovered the theft, Mpiyezintombi would be in other kings' jurisdiction by then.

His biggest regret was that of betraying the trust of the Silent One in the first place. It was trust that had been earned over many years, from as early as the days he sat on his father's knee as a toddler listening to stories of his heroic service to the kingdom. Although at first it was only the songs accompanying the stories that interested him, at the age of about three they began to mean something and became part of him.

His father was a member of iHlaba Regiment under King Dingane kaSenzangakhona. He took pride in the one act that brought universal fame to that regiment – the assassination of the Trek-Boer leader Piet Retief and his men. He narrated with delight how Dingane had initially given Piet Retief tracts of land and how his councillors had objected. Most vocal was the induna of the Ntuli clan, Ndlela kaSompisi. He was the man who took the decision that Retief should be killed.

Retief and his men were invited to join the King in a corralled assembly yard. They were instructed to leave their weapons outside. When the discussion was proceeding, the infantrymen of iHlaba Regiment entered singing a war song. Mpiyezintombi always remembered how his father used to sing a few bars of the chorus as he narrated the story: 'Muntu wami kwaZulu / Wangena! / Wakhuza iwawa / Wangena!' 'My person of kwaZulu / He entered! / He yelled out a war cry / And he entered!'

His father's voice would quiver with excitement at this point.

At the sound of the war cry iwa-w-a-a-a, the men of iHlaba Regiment fell upon the Trek-Boers and beat them to death with sticks and knobkerries. Their Black servants suffered the same fate. All the bodies were dumped in a donga whose banks were then collapsed, burying the dead in a mass grave.

As the son of a man from such a distinguished regiment, Mpiyezintombi was therefore held in high esteem by King Mpande, who succeeded King Dingane, and by Prince Cetshwayo, whose praise poetry included the lines 'Nango ke ozithulele ji, akaqali muntu', 'Here is the silent one, he does not provoke anyone.'

Indeed, the Prince was known as a man who never started conflict. But if anyone dared to provoke him, his response was swift and final. People did not forget how ruthlessly he dealt with his brother-princes when they were bludgeoning one another in some battle of succession.

Six years before his escape from his comrades-in-arms, Mpiyezintombi was a member of the regiment of one thousand and five hundred soldiers who accompanied Prince Cetshwayo, soon after King Mponde's death, on a long march from his homestead in the western region to the capital to claim the throne. The regiment was ready for battle in case any of the other princes got some twisted idea that he was a more rightful heir than Cetshwayo.

This lives in Mpiyezintombi's memory as the most pleasant adventure he has ever undertaken. The entourage included isigodlo girls who carried on their heads all the household items. Their song was echoed by the hills miles away, as were the chants of the warriors and the stamping of their rock-hard soles on the ground. Hundreds of bulls filled the air with their bellowing and, occasionally, some broke away from the herd, running amok and giving the herdboys much joy and laughter as they chased them back into the herd.

Oxen carrying sacks of sorghum followed obediently, as did the heavy-uddered cows that were sulking because they were separated from their calves.

Most memorable were the hunts. The biggest of them was the inqina hunt where Mpiyezintombi and his comrades had to wash their spears in the blood of the gemsbok and other game that they killed as part of the cleansing ritual to remove the misfortune brought about by Mpande's death. The day of the inqina ended excellently for him; he was part of a small group that killed a lion, a rare beast in those parts. It was his spear that found its heart and the beast died immediately without further ado. His spear was therefore washed in the blood of a lion, an honour that followed him for years after that. The Crown Prince was very pleased with his heroism; it augured well for his mission of taking over the throne. He therefore elevated him to command the regiment.

'We know of the great deeds of his father who was a leader of iHlaba Regiment that killed Piet Retief. We can see that, in this case, glowing embers begot other glowing embers instead of ash.'

As he climbed and rappelled the steep cliffs of uK-hahlamba, a cool breeze giving him some respite from the December sun, Mpiyezintombi did not look remotely like anyone whose praise-name was He-Who-Washed-His-Spear-With-The-Blood-Of-A-Lion. He was emaciated and haggard, but he was determined not to give in to exhaustion. The arm of Cetshwayo was so long that it could reach to the end of the earth.

The man he was fleeing was the man for whom he had danced after the long journey to claim the crown had come to an end. At Mlambongwenya Royal Homestead on 1 September 1873, Mpiyezintombi had led his regiment as it rattled the shields and the spears while singing of Ozithulele, yena ongaqali muntu – the Silent One, the one who does not provoke anyone. Women ululated when Theophilus Shepstone, the Secretary for Native Affairs of the Natal government, arrived from Pietermaritzburg, which was the name his people had given to uMgungundlovu, and crowned Cetshwayo the new King of amaZulu.

After Cetshwayo moved to Ondini, where he established his Royal Homestead, Mpiyezintombi was one of four trusted warriors charged with taking care of the King when he did his business on the iNkatha, a sacred work of conceptual art woven into a coil of grass, reeds, supple branches and colourful cloths. It was so respected that common people were not allowed even to mention it.

The iNkatha was kept in eNkatheni, a hut at the centre of the isigodlo that was so private that only the King, the four warriors who took turns looking after him and a venerable old woman who was designated Keeper of the iNkatha were allowed inside. Not even his trusted councillors, his brother-princes or his wives and children could enter eNkatheni. This was also where sacred spears were kept, including the nation's Inhlendla, the barbed sacred spear that was passed from one king of amaZulu to the next, beginning with King Shaka ka-Senzangakhona.

When the King wanted to listen to himself – that is, to brood and introspect – he went to eNkatheni and reposed on the iNkatha in silence and total privacy. However, during important ceremonies, the iNkatha was brought out and the King sat on it in full public gaze. He also sat on it when he was addressing his people on some dire issue that affected the nation, such as a declaration of war or the announcement of a death sentence on some noble personage who had vexed the monarch.

King Cetshwayo also performed his ablution rituals in eNkatheni while sitting on the iNkatha. The four young men took turns to fetch water in glazed clay pots from a well in the distant Hlophekhulu Mountains.

Mpiyezintombi recalled when he saw Nomalanga for the first time. He had come back from the mountain carrying a pot of water and had duly mixed it with sacred herbs to create a rich foam. The Silent One was naked on the iNkatha and was rubbing the foam on his body. Mpiyezintombi was splashing water on his body with a whisk when he thought he saw a shadow in the gap between the reed-woven door and the threshold. He ignored it and continued with his duties. The shadow disappeared briefly.

When it returned, he excused himself, claiming he needed to pee, and rushed outside. Three girls dashed away in different directions as he opened the door. He ran after one of them. When he caught up with the chubby girl, he dragged her behind one of the huts while she protested, 'What do you want with me? I didn't do anything.'

That was Nomalanga, obviously named after the sun because of her bright complexion.

'So, it is true ... this is what you girls do?' said Mpiyezintombi.

He had heard that naughty isigodlo girls liked to take a peep when the King was bathing, but it was the first time he had caught one in the act.

'I didn't do anything,' she said.

'Then why did you run away?'

'Because you were chasing me.'

He threatened to report her to Ozithulele. She begged him not to, all the while smiling as if she didn't really believe he would carry out his threat. Of course, he dared not, for her punishment would be so dire that he wouldn't be able to live with himself afterwards. So he just stood there and allowed himself to be dazzled by the cheeky smile.

That was how the trouble started, resulting in the present situation where his every sneeze, every cough, echoed off the cliffs and the caves of uKhahlamba. No one messed around with isigodlo girls without incurring the wrath of the Silent One. Despite himself, and despite numerous warnings from his comrades-in-arms, Mpiyezintombi had sneaked in a few trysts with her.

An occasional doubt assailed him as he smoked out bees in the crags for their honey, robbed birds' nests of their eggs, or dug out roots and harvested berries. Perhaps he should have stayed and faced the consequences. What could be worse than losing Nomalanga? Execution, the rational side of him said. Execution. He had betrayed the trust of the King, after being elevated to such an eminent position in society.

He remembered how he had once confided in John Dunn, who was a regular visitor and had free access to the isigodlo. He was Cetshwayo's brother-in-law; some of his forty-something amaZulu wives were King Mpande's daughters. Jantoni spoke isiZulu as if he were born into the language and isigodlo girls giggled as he entertained them with stories of a wondrous world called London across the seas, in the land of Queen Victoria, where people travelled in streetcars drawn by horses on iron rails and everyone was White like him except for a few Black faces that could be spotted occasionally in the streets, possibly on some errand for their White masters. He enjoyed the company of isigodlo girls and lay under a tree while they served him sorghum beer, amadumbe, amaqunube berries and roasted game meat. They laughed at his inventive imagination when he described in vivid detail the Metropolitan Railway with its underground electric traction trains.

Though he had married many times, his eye never stopped roaming. In fact, some of his wives were once isigodlo girls who he had spotted and fancied on such visits. He sent delegations with herds of cattle to the Silent One to ask for his wards' hand in marriage, and because he was the King's favourite induna, he always returned with his trophy.

Mpiyezintombi envied him his life of abundance and abandon. Here was a man who could visit his brother-in-law and stay for the whole month just whiling away the time, eating, drinking, telling stories and doing things in the night that Mpiyezintombi could only fantasise about as he lay alone in his hut playing with himself. It was known at the Royal Homestead that Jantoni could have his pick of isigodlo girls any time he felt like it, as if he were the Silent One himself.

When he got tired of this indolence, he rode back to

his own homestead at the coast to do the rounds with his half-White, half-Indonesian wife Catherine, and his more than forty Zulu wives.

Mpiyezintombi vowed that one day he would be like Jantoni. He was already on his way there as one of the military leaders who served the King at the nation's sacred space, where not even Jantoni himself could enter. Soon he would be one of the Silent One's indunas. After that there would be no stopping him.

Mpiyezintombi was taken aback when Jantoni discouraged him from ever entertaining thoughts about an isigodlo girl, particularly Nomalanga. The Silent One already had his eye on her, either for himself or for one of his councillors, generals or indunas as a reward for loyal service. He was waiting for her to ripen a bit more before he made his final decision.

Mpiyezintombi instinctively felt sick at the callous way Jantoni was talking about Nomalanga, as if she was just a fruit hanging on the lowest of branches, waiting to be picked by any passer-by. He remembered the mischievous twinkle in her eye and saw in his mind only a woman of flesh and blood, and of humour and passion, not some succulent produce that must be bargained for and possessed by the highest bidder. He began to suspect that perhaps Jantoni had designs of his own on the young woman.

Mpiyezintombi became very angry at himself for

lacking Jantoni's power and influence. He was impatient. The vultures perching on high branches drooling over Nomalanga would swoop long before he attained the clout that he needed to convince the Silent One that he was a more deserving suitor than any other man, including the Silent One himself. He loved her, and from all indications, she loved him too.

Things had become more difficult for Mpiyezintombi when Nomalanga was transferred from isigodlo esimhlophe – the white isigodlo – a section that contained the huts of the royal children and younger isigodlo girls, to the black isigodlo. The two isigodlos were both at the Royal Homestead but were separated by a palisade fence. The latter contained the King's private house, the huts of his wives and of his mothers – that is, his father's widows – and the elite isigodlo girls who lived in their special hut, called umndlunkulu. The role of these very special isigodlo girls was to serve the King's wives and mothers. Occasionally they serviced the King's needs as concubines.

The King was the only male who had unrestricted access to isigodlo esimnyama – the black isigodlo. His councillors and indunas went there only to hold meetings with him and had to leave immediately after such meetings. An unauthorised male found in the black isigodlo could be executed.

The King's four-walled house, which was built by

Christian converts of sundried bricks and had a thatched roof, was in the black isigodlo. Other building materials such as glass windows, doors, and even a wall mirror were supplied by the Norwegian pastor. It was named indlu emnyama, the black house. It had four rooms, one of which was used by the King to meet his councillors and indunas. Among other tasks, Nomalanga was assigned to clean this house, including the chamber in which the King lounged and ruminated on affairs of state.

At night the black house was guarded by two isigodlo girls who kept its keys; the King slept in his own separate, dome-shaped grass hut.

There were three gates to the isigodlo esimnyama, one of which was reserved for the King, his servants and isigodlo girls. The second gate was for use only by his birth-mother when she was still alive, and by her most senior co-wife after the birth-mother's death. The third gate was for the rest of the wives and mothers.

It was with the connivance of the two girls that Mpi-yezintombi sneaked into the black isigodlo using the King's gate and had a tryst with Nomalanga in the black house. All four of these young people were risking their lives; girls had been executed for lesser crimes. For instance, the story was told of how the King ordered the execution of two girls who had failed in their duties to feed the banker masons and bricklayers who were constructing the black house. And there were men who had been caught associating with the royal wives and were taken to the execution place at the banks of the Umfolozi River, where strong men twisted their necks in a spiral until they were dead.

Nomalanga was worth the risk.

One afternoon Mpiyezintombi was woken from a reverie by the music of the reed pipes, a significant occurrence, for they had been silent for the entire year. He knew at once that they were proclaiming the new year. The King had tasted the new harvest and the populace was now allowed to eat the season's new crops.

After leaving the barracks – which consisted of several dome-shaped grass huts separated from the white isigodlo by a palisade fence – he joined the rest of the warriors in the festivities, dances and such rituals as the mass bathing in the river.

This was such an important festival that even the White missionaries attended it. So did John Dunn, whose whiteness qualified him to be referred to as umfundisi – pastor – by some ignorant villagers. The White folk all sat with the Silent One enjoying his favourite food of curdled milk, amadumbe cocoyams, wild spinach, roasted meat and sorghum beer.

This was the only time people could speak while the King was eating. Normally there would be silence in the whole of the Royal Homestead when the King was having his meal. An announcement would be made by his grooms, who would go around the Royal Homestead shouting, 'Ungathinti! Do not touch! Do not disturb! The King is eating!' One could not even cough until the announcement was made that the King had eaten to his satisfaction. But today, because of the presence of the White men, things were different. People talked, laughed and even coughed as the Silent One and his guests gourmandised.

Mpiyezintombi knew that though the White men's presence was ostensibly to enjoy the first fruits with the King and to pay their respects to him, their crucial mission was to convince him to accede to the ultimatum Sir Bartle Frere had sent early that December, that King Cetshwayo should dismantle his military system or face a war with the British.

The reason given was that some of his warriors constantly crossed uThukela River to kill British subjects on the Natal side of the border. The King knew, of course, that the real intention was to contain the military might of the amaZulu nation.

He told Jantoni and the missionaries that he was the King and could not be given ultimatums by servants of other monarchs – Frere was the British High Commissioner for Southern Africa. This was the same response the Silent One had given to Frere's messengers.

Mpiyezintombi found this very exciting, as did his fellow amabutho. Their spears and muskets were thirsty for British blood. Warriors become restless and fidgety without war.

At sunset the merry-making was over. The missionaries rode back to their mission stations and Jantoni repaired to the guest hut, where isigodlo girls would be pampering him, serving him victuals and their bodies if the activities of the day and intoxication had left some stamina in him.

The King first went to eNkatheni to sit on the iNkatha and commune with ancestral spirits. And then he went to his hut, where he was supposed to sleep by himself. He was required to abstain from women this night. He was said to be fasting.

In the evening Mpiyezintombi was skulking near the King's gate, which was closest to the black house, when he heard the familiar whistling. He entered the gate and walked uprightly and brazenly to the black house so that whoever might be lurking in the shadows would think he had legitimate business there. Nomalanga was waiting outside the door, but the girls with the keys were nowhere to be found. He surmised that they had been carried away with the festivities and neglected their duty of guarding the black house. The lovers hid behind the bushes that grew near the house.

'We must elope,' said Mpiyezintombi. 'Not immediately, but soon after the war. I still need to taste some real action against the British.'

'He-Who-Washed-His-Spear-With-The-Blood-Of-A-Lion now wants to wash it with the blood of the White man?'

'The blade of my spear has earned it,' said Mpiyezintombi, his voice filled with braggadocio.

'How do you know you'll come back alive?' asked Nomalanga with a giggle.

'No soldier goes to war to die.'

Mpiyezintombi waited for a while for her response. When none was forthcoming he nudged her and said, 'I will not let the Silent One gift you to anyone. Not even to himself. We must elope.'

'We can't,' said Nomalanga. 'That would disgrace my father.'

Mpiyezintombi understood exactly what she meant. Isigodlo girls were daughters of amaZulu nobility and military generals who caught the eye of the King and were ceded to him. It was a sad experience for the parents to part with their daughters, and yet a great honour at the same time. The shame would be not only hers but her parents', too, if she eloped with another man. Nomalanga would certainly not want to do anything that would disgrace her father or jeopardise his life. One never knew what form the wrath of the Silent One would take.

Mpiyezintombi suddenly shushed Nomalanga; he thought he heard female voices coming from the direction of the King's hut.

'Is the Silent One not supposed to be fasting?' whispered Mpiyezintombi.

'Maybe it's the royal mothers,' said Nomalanga. 'They are supposed to guard his hut when he is fasting.'

'They were not there. I waited for you for a long time and saw no one.'

Mpiyezintombi panicked when the women's voices became louder and were joined by the King's. He had imagined the rest of the black isigodlo were asleep at that hour. He asked Nomalanga to lie flat on the ground among the bushes while he sneaked out to investigate.

He saw two isigodlo girls armed with muskets guarding the King. He was wearing his black overcoat with red trimmings on the sleeves and collar, and a black hat and shoes. This was the special attire that he wore only when he went to caca on the mound with latticed reed fencing that he used as a latrine. On every occasion he went to evacuate his bowels he assumed the guise of a British officer. The guards stood to attention at the entrance while the Silent One did his business.

Mpiyezintombi marvelled at the guards. It was a new custom altogether. Ordinarily when the King was fasting, he was guarded by the royal mothers, who would be unarmed. The practice of having girls armed with guns began only with the new rumours of an imminent war with the British. Older isigodlo girls known as amakhikiza had been formed into a regiment and were taught how to use firearms. Nomalanga was one of them and she told Mpiyezintombi that they were the new home-guard for the King, who had more confidence in them than in the men.

Mpiyezintombi became careless; he tripped on a stone and fell. The guards spotted him as he tried to creep back to join Nomalanga.

'Who goes there?' shouted one.

He was sure she had seen him but hoped she couldn't identify him. At that time the Silent One was standing at the latticed entrance and Mpiyezintombi had no choice but to flee. As he pushed the gate open, the King shouted, 'I have seen you, son of Khabazela. What witchcraft are you doing at the black house this time of the night?'

Mpiyezintombi cursed the moon. Of course, as one of the warriors who splashed him with sacred water during the iNkatha ceremonies, the Silent One would be able to recognise him even from his silhouette.

He took to his heels with nothing but his spear and his shield, which he always carried with him. He was certain that in the morning the King would summon him. Perhaps he would even send armed guards to frog-march him to his royal presence. He should be nowhere to be found by then. There would be no quarter given to anyone suspected of witchcraft. He-Who-Washed-His-Spear-With-The-Blood-Of-A-Lion fled like a feather being blown by a relentless wind, abandoning the comforts of his warrior life, and the respect and honour he had enjoyed from his peers and from his liege.

The possibility of war with the British was taken seriously. Mpiyezintombi's regiment was hard in training, practising various manoeuvres, as were other regiments. As he ran across the valleys and up the hills he regretted that he would miss the war, the opportunity to distinguish himself in his regiment by slaying the British.

He hoped Nomalanga would have enough sense to lie there silently, and when the Silent One was back in his hut and all was quiet again, sneak back to umndlunkulu undetected. The Silent One would never know he had turned the black house into a trysting place. Let him continue believing he was alone doing some witchcraft there. Let him engage his best medicine men, diviners and shamans to neutralise whatever harmful magical potions he believed Mpiyezintombi had planted at the black house.

3

London – April 1880
The Great Farini

Em-Pee stands at the dock in Liverpool holding a jute sack of his worldly possessions, including his victuals for the voyage – salted pork and hard biscuits. The rest of his colleagues, all of them professing to be Zulus except Slaw, who is the only White man in the troupe, hold similar sacks and stand in trepidation among the buzz of boisterous Irishmen excited at immigrating to America.

Steerage is waiting for them and the troupe is not looking forward to it. Most of them have experienced it before. Slightly more than a year ago they sailed in steerage from Cape Town to London. Em-Pee remembers how he got seasick and threw up a few times. He hopes it will not happen this time; his body must by now be inured to the rigours of sea travel. He is grateful that the crossing from Liverpool to New York is said to be much shorter than that voyage of many weeks. It will take only about ten days in the iron-hulled steamship.

His eyes search for The Great Farini in the crowd but he is nowhere to be seen. The gangplank has been lowered to the dock but only cabin passengers have boarded. Perhaps he is already resting comfortably in his first-class cabin.

'Why the long face? This is the big time, guv.'

That is Slaw standing next to him with a big grin, crunching potato crisps. Em-Pee likes Czeslaw Trzetrzelewska. Like Mpiyezintombi, his name is quite a mouthful to the lazy tongues of the English, so they just call him Slaw. The Great Farini, however, mastered Slaw's name and relishes calling him Mister Trzetrzelewska. Em-Pee has always wondered why he never took the same trouble to master Mpiyezintombi. He once voiced that concern. The Great Farini merely looked at him, shook his head and chuckled. Em-Pee gave up and grudgingly accepted the corruption of his name. He was to accept many other things after that, at first grudgingly, but by and by they would become part of who he was.

He has since learned to embrace and love the name.

'P.T. Barnum is the Greatest Show on Earth,' says Slaw.

'I know,' says Em-Pee.

Slaw looks at him closely, wondering why he is not evincing the slightest sign of excitement. 'We're going to be in it, guv. We're going to be in the Greatest Show on Earth.'

Going to America has been Slaw's biggest dream from the time he joined The Great Farini and tasted the thrill of performance. He never imagined he would be in a circus one day. Never had ambition to be anything but the street hustler he had always been until Em-Pee rescued him from sleeping rough and changed his life.

The Greatest Show on Earth means nothing to Em-Pee. He has heard a lot about it, but has never envisaged a life as a circus performer. A formal circus, that is, with giant marquees, clowns, trapeze artists, performing animals and candy floss. The dances that he and a whole bunch of 'Zulus' imported from Africa perform for The Great Farini don't really qualify as a circus. The boss calls them 'human curiosity spectacles' and they often feature what less erudite impresarios call 'freak show' staples such as Daughter of Hottentot Venus, a young Khoikhoi girl with a big bottom and drooping breasts captured in the wilds of the Cape of Good Hope and adored by audiences for her resemblance to the original Hottentot Venus, born Sara Baartman, as seen in the sketches on the posters displayed at performances. The word that went around, never discounted by The Great Farini, was that the Khoikhoi girl was the authentic daughter of Baartman. Londoners never questioned how it was possible for Baartman, who died in 1815 in Paris at the age of twenty-five, to have an eighteen-year-old daughter in London in 1879 – sixty-four years later.

Unlike other curiosities in Farini's menagerie, Daughter of Hottentot Venus does not exert herself performing contortions and grotesqueries. She just stands on a chair naked, with only a string of cowrie shells around her waist. Audiences line up to examine her big bottom, huge thighs and her elongated labia minora, which hang between the thighs, while they listen to a lecture on steatopygia, a genetic condition found among the native women of the southern tip of Africa, which endows them with oversized genitalia and derrières. The Great Farini believes very strongly in education, and all the performances are accompanied by lectures about the exotic places and cultures of the performers. Serious members of the audience take notes and make sketches as they inspect the woman's parts closely. In the name of decency and of respecting the woman's privacy, The Great Farini never allows the audience to touch her. There is a sign on her pedestal: *Do Not Touch The Exhibit.*

This voyage may be welcome to adventure-seekers like Slaw, but the departure from the shores of England leaves Em-Pee with unexplained poignancy. Perhaps it is because the voyage takes him further and further away from Cape Town, and therefore from kwaZulu, to which he still yearns to return. A year is a long time, a lot has happened, and his sins should also be forgiven, though his people have a saying that a crime once committed does not decay.

The memory of his escape from the consequences of that crime doesn't decay either. It is as fresh as if it happened only last month. Yet it was almost two years ago that he traversed rugged landscapes, climbing mountains and abseiling steep cliffs, crossing deep gorges, overflowing rivers, luxuriant meadows and arid wastelands from bucolic Ondini, where birdsong wove itself into the refrains of the maidens bathing and washing clothes at the river, to the bustling impersonality of the city of Cape Town. He had arrived there after months of trekking south-westwards, living on roots and rodents and the occasional kindness of strangers. Sometimes he would be fortunate enough to hitch a ride on a wagon in a trader's caravan in exchange for his labour, or would assist in harvesting prickly pears in the Karoo, and in shearing merinos. He chortles when he recalls how he twice escaped with his life from bloodthirsty highwaymen, on one occasion facing two of them and fighting them with his assegai until they took to their heels. But on another occasion he took to the hills himself because there were too many attackers to take on.

In the big city by the sea he slept rough for a while, doing part-time work in the manicured gardens of Rondebosch, until he was employed to clean and cook at a homeless shelter by a Captain of the Hallelujah Army, a missionary group founded by William and Catherine Booth in England 'to meet human needs in Christ's name without discrimination'. The church had recently set up in Cape Town and was gaining many followers, especially among the destitute and the hungry, by feeding them; but also by singing, playing drums and trumpets, dancing and preaching in the streets in their black and red military uniforms. Those who knew real soldiers who fought real wars laughed at their pretension to militarism – uniforms, ranks and all. The missionaries ignored the mirth, declaring themselves to be soldiers, albeit of salvation.

The Captain liked Mpiyezintombi's work ethic so much that he decided to employ him on a full-time basis, and gave him a room in his backyard and hand-me-down clothes from members of the congregation. Thus, he discarded his traditional ibheshu and impala-skin kaross, and strutted around in brown riding breeches, a pleated-bib pullover shirt and elastic-sided boots.

The Captain encouraged him to attend a night school in the docklands run by the same Christian army and was impressed to see that he had a great flair for language. Within months he could read and understand basic English, though the writing lagged. The Captain encouraged him to read his *Cape Argus* before he disposed of the newspapers in a disused basement where they were stored in stacks tied with twine, gathering mould that filled the place with musty odours.

Mpiyezintombi Mkhize learned of the events in kwa-Zulu from the excitement in his master's household. The wire services brought news from Natal of a fermenting Anglo-Zulu War.

The Captain had been disillusioned with the increasingly liberal stance of the *Cape Argus*, which openly advocated integration. He was now an ardent reader of *The Lantern*, a weekly pro-imperialist paper that Mpiyezintombi devoured with much enthusiasm because of its funny cartoons and caricatures of the liberals it opposed.

It was from the pages of *The Lantern* that Mpiyezintombi learned of the amaZulu victory at the Battle of Isandlwana. He later confirmed it with his master, and again with the teacher and fellow students at the docklands night school. Piecing snatches of stories together, he re-created the battle in his imagination as if he were there himself. All the while he regretted that his desire for Nomalanga had deprived him of the opportunity to share in the glory of annihilating the British.

The British colonists in Natal had finally carried out their threat and crossed uThukela River to attack the kwaZulu Kingdom. Mpiyezintombi remembered how Sir Bartle Frere, the British High Commissioner for Southern Africa and therefore a personal representative of the Great White Queen from across the seas, had given King Cetshwayo kaMpande a silly ultimatum even before he, Mpiyezintombi, had escaped from Ondini. He'd known that his king would ignore it, but he didn't believe the English would be so foolish as to invade his people.

The Red Coats, led by Lieutenant General Lord Chelmsford, marched into the Kingdom of amaZulu, creating havoc in their path, particularly on crops and livestock. Women and children took to the hills, and all menfolk, except for the very old and sickly, took their places in their various regiments.

The ever-so-liberal *Cape Argus*, reporting on this invasion, wrote of a speech recalled by those present, where Cetshwayo addressed his soldiers and said in a plaintive voice, 'I have not gone over the seas to look for the White man, yet they have come into my country and I would not be surprised if they took away our wives and cattle and crops and land. I have nothing against the White man and I cannot tell why they came to me. What shall I do?'

When Mpiyezintombi read these words, he sighed deeply and a single tear dropped down his cheek. At the mention of the women who would be taken away as if they were part of the cattle and land, his mind darted to Nomalanga. She would never allow herself to be taken, he assured himself. Yet he wondered where she could be. She had been one of the isigodlo girls who had been armed with muskets and were acting as the king's personal bodyguards. Could Cetshwayo have sent them into battle? He remembered her as a very feisty woman. She would fight to the death if any British soldier tried to abduct her.

On the eleventh day, on 22 January 1879, the Red Coats faced Cetshwayo's troops. The amaZulu military formations were under the supreme command of a general of whom Mpiyezintombi was in awe, Ntshingwa-yo kaMahole Khoza – one of the men who had mentored him through the ranks.

Mpiyezintombi knew that he would have led one of the regiments if he had been there. Indeed, a mate of his, a man who served under him once, Mavumengwana kaNdlela, was basking in the glory of having led the regiment that administered the lethal blow to Chelmsford's well-resourced army.

The British Empire fell to its knees that day at the Battle of Isandlwana. A force of twenty thousand soldiers armed only with cowhide shields, short assegais and a few muskets, destroyed columns of one thousand and eight hundred Red Coats armed with the latest in military technology – Martini-Henry breech-loaders, field guns and Hale rocket batteries. More than one thousand and three hundred Red Coats were killed that day, and the rest were put to flight.

Mpiyezintombi narrated to his classmates the details of the battle as if he had been there himself. After all, he was part of the command structure that had planned the manoeuvres in readiness for the British attack. For this reason, his heart bled even more that he had missed the action. All thanks to Nomalanga.

His classmates took his stories with more than just a pinch of salt. He was in Cape Town when this battle was fought. How could he know so much about it? Even narrating the arguments that ensued after the British had fled? He surely was a man of rich imagination, which did not surprise them in the least. After all, he had learned to read and write and speak the language of the White man with so much skill that the teacher, a doddering retired Lieutenant of the Hallelujah Army, left him to mind the class when he had other errands to run or was otherwise indisposed.

It was during those moments that he re-enacted the battle, emitting war cries that would have curdled the blood of the most hot-blooded British warrior, and dancing the victory dance. When the teacher returned in the middle of such performances, he would not stop them but would watch till the final applause. Then he would join the debate as to whether Cetshwayo was correct in not pursuing the British across the river into Natal. Mpiye-zintombi felt quite bitter that the military might of ama-Zulu stopped at the river, as the king expressly forbade the incursion into what had become British territory. He knew that his comrades-in-arms, especially Mavumeng-wana kaNdlela, would have urged the king to make the most of the victory by rooting out Chelmsford's forces in the colonial settlements and farms, and taking those lands back into the fold of the kwaZulu Kingdom.

'The British did not come with any land from England,' said Mpiyezintombi. 'Every bit of what you call Natal once belonged to my ancestors.'

'Cetewayo is wise,' said the teacher, using the English corruption of the king's name. 'It is a kingly gesture, as even the *Argus* has reported. It is the only way to sue for peace and establish good neighbourly relations with us. If he violated that border, things would be worse. It would be the end of his kingdom.'

The teacher was drawing the line as an Englishman, though of a liberal ilk, and including himself among those who felt they had a justifiable stake in Natal. He was English and Mpiyezintombi was Zulu.

'Why should we sue for peace? We won the war. We should take the spoils. They belong to us in any case.'

'You didn't win a war; you won a battle. Obviously Cetewayo is wiser than you'll ever be. That's why he is king and you're here, a thousand miles away, scraping a living in the docklands.'

Mpiyezintombi retreated into a grudging silence that lasted many days. The teacher seemed amused by his sulk and continued with his lessons. Until one day when the teacher called him to his desk after class and showed him the previous day's *Cape Argus*. William Hunt was back in town. The teacher explained that he was a North American man, famous for walking across Niagara Falls on a tightrope in his native Canada, and as part of a group of trapeze artists called the Flying Farinis who had travelled to many countries performing gymnastic feats.

He had since retired as a performer and was a

successful impresario who had curated some of the most amazing ethnographic displays and performances in London. He called himself The Great Farini, and he had come to this part of Africa looking for performers and exhibits for his human curiosity spectacles. He was returning from the Kalahari, where he had discovered the famous Lost City, with a family of Kalahari Bushmen who were going to be part of his display of primitive races. He was keen to get a few Zulu men, Cetewayo's warriors who had defeated the most powerful army in the world, and take them with him to London.

'He'd better go to kwaZulu if he wants men who fought at Isandlwana,' said Mpiyezintombi.

'You are from there,' said the teacher. 'You can be of assistance to this man, and maybe earn yourself a few quid.'

It was not difficult for the teacher to locate The Great Farini at a boarding house in Claremont. Mpiyezintombi was struck by his singular look, quite different from any White man he had seen in Cape Town or back home in kwaZulu. He must have been in his early forties, with a long black beard, an imperial moustache waxed so that it stood out long and straight like a pencil on either side of his face, a long black cape over a black suit, a black top hat – everything about him was dark, like a character who had just walked out of the pages of a Varney the Vampire story.

The Great Farini was excited to hear Mpiyezintombi's story. He was just the man he was looking for.

For the first time Mpiyezintombi learned that Cetshwayo was quite a celebrity in England for his defeat of the British army. This did not make sense to him. How could the British celebrate their own defeat? They were indeed strange creatures. The British admired bravery, Farini explained. A group of primitive Zulus chanting their war dances would be a hit, and the performers would make a lot of money.

It didn't take much to convince Mpiyezintombi to join The Great Farini. Four more men – dockworkers in their day jobs – were recruited from the night school. It did not matter that some were not Zulus. The British would not know the difference.

In March 1879 they set off, spending about two months sailing in steerage to England. Mpiyezintombi spent most of the voyage teaching the men how to be Zulus, between bouts of seasickness. He also spent a lot of time drumming it into his own head, as Farini had instructed, that he had indeed personally fought at Isandlwana and killed a few British soldiers with his assegai, and that he was in fact a Zulu prince, son of King Cetshwayo himself.

The assegai and shield he had brought with him when he escaped came in handy.

* * *

Slaw, Em-Pee and the rest of the troupe are settled between decks. Em-Pee's special assegai and shield are safely packed with the drums, the costumes of tiger and leopard skins, ostrich and peacock feathers and the rest of the performance paraphernalia in the cargo hold of the ship.

The crate contains more spears forged for Farini by blacksmiths in London for use by the rest of the Zulus, and shields shaped by the performers themselves from cowhides bought at an abattoir and horse hides from a glue factory.

The Zulus have lived together as Zulus for one year; it has long become irrelevant that two of them are amaXhosa and one is an Owambo man. There is only one other man, Samson, who has any genuine claim to Zuluness. Now they are all amaZulu, even among themselves, as much as they are Zulus to the spectators. Perhaps one day, when they get back home, if they ever do, they will resume their various ethnic identities. They long bonded under the leadership of Em-Pee, who attained that status naturally as a genuine Cetshwayo warrior and faux prince who also was wise to the ways of the White man due to his ability to read and speak his language.

In steerage, the Zulus in their khaki uniforms huddle together on straw mattresses near the long tables that separate the front bunks reserved for single men from the middle ones that are for families. Single women have their bunks further aft.

The Irish emigrants hog all the berths to themselves, and they eye the Zulus suspiciously. The Zulus return the gaze nonchalantly. The emigrants are mostly men, but there are quite a few families – that is, husband, wife and kids. There is also a handful of women who were on their own initially, but some have now loosely paired with single men or have joined the merrymaking over rum with a group of swashbucklers.

In the first two days of the voyage, the Zulus were happy to take a rest from their hectic schedule of daily performances. They enjoyed lazing about on the mattresses while occasionally nibbling on their provisions. And listening to the rum-fuelled songs of the Irishmen. But now their legs are itching for action. The restricted walks between decks give very little respite.

* * *

It is an understatement to characterise the performances as hectic. In the beginning, they were only once a day at the glass-roofed Royal Westminster Aquarium, endearingly called the Aq by its patrons, in downtown London. Thousands of spectators flocked to see their favourites, such as Zazel the human cannonball shot out of a cannon by The Great Farini himself, who would stand there in his Gothic suit and cape and wicked beard and, to the beat of drums and blare of bugles. The cannon would shoot the beautiful Zazel out right across the hall into a net that Farini himself had invented. In fact, he claimed that this whole act was of his origination. Crowds went wild as Zazel flew over their heads, men raising their top hats in awe and women screeching with excitement.

There were quite a few other amazing performances and displays of human and non-human curiosities. For instance, there was the Two-Headed Nightingale, African-American conjoined twins imported from North Carolina who sang in two-part harmony and danced an awkward jig. Some of the favourites were frightening gorillas from the forests of Africa, clownish midgets, and, of course, Daughter of Hottentot Venus.

And then there were the Zulus.

The Great Farini would stride on to the stage and announce, 'Ladies and gentlemen, and now for the highlight of the day, the ferocious Zulus. Yes, the very warriors of the Battle of Isandlwana, who killed eight hundred of the Empire's bravest soldiers under the leadership of their savage king, Cetewayo!'

At this point Cetshwayo was a celebrity in Britain, and the mention of his name provoked cheers of admiration as well as boos of loathing from the audience.

This was the cue for Em-Pee to lead his men on to

the stage, screaming and kicking their legs, throwing themselves to the floor, rolling their eyes and baring their blood-soaked teeth, flicking their tongues enhanced with deep-red dye and emitting blood-curdling war chants. All this to the frenzy of the drums. Audiences of thousands would be mesmerised and recoil in fear. Sometimes the Zulus would jump off the stage and dash among the audience, waving their shields and assegais as the people cringed in terror. Those macho men in the company of ladies would take a stance that clearly indicated that they were prepared to fight back if the savages dared to attack them.

Em-Pee hated this performance intensely. In the beginning, even as they were between decks on their voyage from Cape Town to Britain, he had taught the men proper Zulu dances, very rhythmic, orderly and beautifully choreographed. But The Great Farini banned those dances. Though they comprised aggressive foot-stomping and the dancers throwing themselves violently to the ground, all this was done in a graceful and deliberate manner. It was not savage enough. The British audiences would not buy it. He wanted the Zulus to perform in a disorderly, noisy and chaotic manner, screaming and jumping about as befitting savages.

The Great Farini paid the piper, so he called the tune. Even though it was discordant to Em-Pee's ears, he had to go along with it. Sometimes the performers would sneak in dance movements from their various ethnic groups, but as soon as Farini saw that they were becoming too beautiful, he would warn them, 'You cannot have beautiful dances, you are savages; otherwise you'll alienate the audiences; everything about you must be ugly.'

To the audiences the Zulu dancers represented authentic Africa, the epicentre of man-eating barbarism. They were the mythical beasts butchering British sons and fathers in exotic lands far, far away. And here, The Great Farini had brought them to life in front of their eyes, compelling them to face the monstrosity. Ever the educationist, this wonderful impresario would begin the performances by strutting across the stage and reading, with much dramatic flair, a letter from Sir Theophilus Shepstone, the Secretary for Native Affairs in Natal, attesting that the men were genuine Zulus placed by him, a servant of Her Majesty's Government, in the custody of The Great Farini, and that one of them was the son of the Zulu principal chief, Cetewayo of Isandlwana infamy. These men had fought in that battle, and each one's assegai was stained with the blood of Englishmen.

Sometimes the assegais were taken to the streets. The Zulus in their ostrich and peacock feathers and tiger skins would prance up and down Hyde Park Corner, attracting curious onlookers, with a barker loudhailing prospective spectators to come and witness the height of titillating savagery at St George's Gallery. Titillation was a big part of The Great Farini's philosophy of entertainment. So was education. A good show educated the audience about the primitive races and their cultures, thrilled them with their performances and traditions, and, most importantly, offended and outraged the audiences with their manners and practices, or even their looks. It was from the outrage that titillation came. The naked parts of Daughter of Hottentot Venus. The warrior bodies of the Zulus that radiated pulsating maleness.

The erotic charge that The Great Farini injected into his exhibits was so popular that the Zulus had to perform their routine three or four times a day. And each routine was becoming longer as the impresario thought of more items to add to keep the audiences coming. The new favourite was a demonstration of how the Zulus killed their enemies. It was so thrilling that newspapers wrote about it, the *London Times* reporting that the savages' method of killing their victims was so real it struck terror 'into the stoutest heart' and 'the fiendish reality of their war dances and songs is marvellous in its true and horrible intensity'.

Farini was good at conjuring innovative ways of promoting the show. On one occasion, for instance, he took them to the London Zoo, where they marvelled at wild animals in their cages. Newspaper reporters were on hand to record for posterity as Em-Pee shed a tear at the sight of so majestic a creature as a lion confined behind iron bars instead of roaming the wilds. But the Zulus were also intrigued by many other animals they had never seen before in their country, such as Bengal tigers, pumas and grizzly bears. The next day newspapers had pictures of the Zulus at the zoo with captions on how they blended so well and were at home in an environment that must have made them nostalgic for their country.

Such publicity stunts introduced the spectacles to wider audiences; the Aq was packed, and Farini added more items to the repertoire.

'You are killing us with work, Farini,' said Em-Pee when the impresario had finally agreed to give him an audience after weeks of requesting a meeting. 'My mates have sent me to ask for a raise. Either you cut down the number of shows we have to do per day or you pay us more.'

'What is this, Em-Pee?' asked Farini. 'I feed you people. I give you accommodation. I can't afford to pay you more. I am losing a lot of money.'

'The venues are always full.'

'That's how it looks to you. But you don't know the expenses. And now I am losing Matilda. You know how much money I am going to lose when Matilda leaves?'

Em-Pee did not know who Matilda was, and he said so.

'Miss Rossa Matilda Richter. Zazel.'

'Zazel? Zazel is leaving?'

'She's going to America. She's joining P.T. Barnum. I need a replacement as of yesterday. And you come with your money problems?'

'You can shoot one of us from the cannon,' said Em-Pee jokingly.

'For more money, of course. That's all you people think about.'

'Yes, the same salary you were giving Zazel.'

Farini's imperial moustache twitched.

'Thanks for offering, but it would not work,' he said. 'Who gives a damn if a native dies?'

'I do,' said Em-Pee.

'I do too, old chap. You know you're all my friends. More like family. But the spectators don't see things that way. We need somebody Caucasoid. Someone they empathise with and therefore fear for her life. They must root for her safety because she looks like them. They don't want her to get hurt. You shoot a Negro from a cannon, no one gives a hoot. They don't see it as anything to marvel at. He's from a different world, some may even think a subhuman world. In their minds the Negro is made of different stuff. We need a beautiful, frail White person. A woman is much better. Or a man disguised as a woman. They are interested in her survival, so the whole performance grabs their emotions and they hold their breath until she falls safely in the net.'

It was the kind of diatribe Em-Pee did not understand. He stopped listening at Caucasoid, a term he had heard at Farini's anthropology lectures before the performances, often contrasted with Negroid and Mongoloid.

The Zulus decided to give The Great Farini some breathing space while he looked for Zazel's replacement.

'You tell him only until he finds Zazel's replacement,' said Samson as they walked to their quarters at the Devil's Acre near Westminster Abbey.

As usual, the darkest London loafers sleeping rough after befuddling and numbing themselves in opium dens hollered a few choice expletives at them. 'Hey, Sambo, how many White explorers have you eaten today?'

'Sambo is your father's whore pipe!' Em-Pee hollered back. The other Zulus joined in with expletives of their own, mostly about the private parts of the loafers' mothers. This meant nothing to the loafers; they merely laughed. One ragamuffin was particularly loud, following the Zulus and yelling something about blackamoors. He was a familiar nuisance to the Zulus. They cracked a few jokes about his being an emaciated fleabag and walked on.

A vintage landau dropped an elderly couple dressed in tattered clothes and rode away. Their mode of transport and well-fed pampered faces gave them away at once. They were well-heeled Londoners from exclusive neighbourhoods who relished visiting the slums to immerse themselves in poverty and grime and then, after the dirty weekend, returned to their lives of luxury. Em-Pee joked that if he had that kind of money he would not be seen dead in the slums.

Some slummers came just to satisfy their curiosity about how the other half lived, others to dispense charity. Young gentlemen slummers, however, were really tot-hunting, looking for what they called dirty puzzle. Or just seeking degenerate amusements of other kinds, such as opium dens.

The emaciated ragamuffin redirected his attention from the Zulus to the elderly couple. Suddenly he became a pitiful figure. With hands cupped, he begged for money. The gentleman addressed him as if he was some cute pet, patted him on the head and ruffled his dirty hair. He took a coin from his pocket and gave it to him.

But the ragamuffin was not interested in the coin; he knew exactly where to reach into the threadbare waistcoat to grab a pocket watch before dashing away, with the watch chain twirling in the light of the street gas lamps. The gentleman staggered and fell.

Em-Pee ran after the ragamuffin while the other Zulus went to assist the couple. There was no way an emaciated street urchin could outrun a Zulu warrior. The boy cursed and screamed as Em-Pee grabbed him by the scruff of the neck and brought him back to his victim. He forced him to give the watch back and apologise.

Em-Pee was struck by the ragamuffin's soft features. He could easily be a girl. An idea hit him. This could be the new Zazel. It would just take some work to scrub off all the filth, make him up and dress him as a girl.

It did take some convincing, but with the promise not to call the coppers on him and instead give him the opportunity for stardom, he allowed himself to be led into the presence of The Great Farini by the blackamoors. The impresario bought the idea, and young Czeslaw Trzetrzelewska, alias Slaw, became a member of Farini's troupe. He was made up into a lady and shot from a cannon.

But he was also used for other roles. As he grew big and strong with good feeding, his skin was darkened with black cork, and he became a native of some invented Indian Ocean islands. Sometimes he was painted brown with shoe polish and pitted against Mpiyezintombi in the battle of the savage races where, as a tiny but powerful warrior, he felled the giant Zulu in a David-and-Goliath confrontation.

As soon as Slaw was settled in his routine as Zazel II, the Zulus resumed their demand for a raise and improved work conditions. The Great Farini felt aggrieved that they were continuing with their ingratitude.

And then Ulundi happened, adding to his woes.

The news came in dribs and drabs. No one had believed the greatest military force in the world would allow savages to get away with victory, yet no one expected Chelmsford's revenge would happen so soon and so swiftly. On 4 July 1879, only six months after Isandlwana, a force of twenty thousand Zulu soldiers was brought to its knees by seventeen thousand Red Coats of Her Majesty the Queen and their allies.

Em-Pee was sitting outside a marquee giving reading and writing lessons to Slaw. He was proud of the young man; he was catching on very fast. Slaw had resisted at first because he had not believed that a Black man from Africa could teach him anything, but he had since gained more respect for his 'guv', as he had then taken to addressing Em-Pee.

The Great Farini came scampering towards them, waving a sheaf of papers.

'Maybe he is going to offer you more money, guv,' said Slaw softly.

It was meant only for Em-Pee's ears but Farini heard him. He perched himself next to them. 'That is all you can think of? Money?'

'Just a joke, sir, Mr Great Farini,' said Slaw.

'We have more problems than your demands for more money,' said Farini, brandishing the papers in Em-Pee's face. 'Your people have let us down. They were thoroughly defeated at the Battle of Ulundi. That's not good for my business. Who will pay to watch defeated savages?'

He read for them from *The Evening Star* on 'The Capture of Ulundi'. A smarting Lord Chelmsford had ordered the return of four hundred and fourteen cattle Cetshwayo had sent to Natal in his attempt to sue for peace. Instead he sent Her Majesty's forces, numbering thousands of Europeans and hundreds of natives, to raze the Zulu Kingdom at its very heart.

By noon Ulundi was in flames, and during the day all the military kraals of the Zulu army in the valley of Umvolosi were destroyed.

One would have thought there would be joy in Farini's voice as he read this. But no, there was sadness. Em-Pee experienced even more sadness but did not want to show it.

The only excited person was Slaw. As Farini read, he screamed, 'Give 'em hell, Charley, give 'em hell! Batty-fang 'em, John Bull!'

Farini, on the other hand, was struck by the discovery that there were natives who fought on the side of the British and therefore the British could not claim all the glory. As he read on, he discovered that in the cavalry were five hundred mounted Basotho men under Colonel Chrode.

'The king! What do they say happened to King Cetshwayo?' asked Em-Pee, agitated. He was sad that he could hear of this war only from the side of the British and their war correspondents. He yearned to get the side of his people.

Farini skimmed through the papers looking for news of the Zulu king.

There is no further news of Cetewayo, who left Ulundi on the 3rd inst. The Natal Witness *publishes the following description of the battle by the correspondent of the* London Daily Telegraph*: – The British marched in hollow square, the 8th regiment and Gatlin battery forming with the 90th regiment ...*

Farini stopped right there. He was not interested in the details of how the battle was fought and won, or how the Zulus were flying before the advancing cavalry, bolting up the mountain until they were out of reach. Like Em-Pee, but for different reasons, he was interested in the fate of Cetshwayo.

'If Cetewayo dies, the Zulus lose their shine. If the Zulus lose their shine, you can kiss your job goodbye,' said Farini, as he stood up abruptly and scurried away.

'Thank heavens I am not a Zulu, guv,' said Slaw. 'The cannon doesn't depend on any war.'

'You are becoming too fat for the cannon,' said Em-Pee. 'You may kiss your job goodbye too.'

Later they learned that Cetshwayo had not been killed. He had gone into hiding but was captured a month later. Em-Pee's eyes were misty with unshed tears when he saw a newspaper picture of him with his jailers. He was not in chains, as one would expect of a prisoner, but was standing majestically in front of a cannon on the Cape of Good Hope Castle ramparts, wearing a well-tailored European suit and hat. Next to him were his custodian, Captain Ruscombe Poole, and his interpreter, Henry Longcast, who was leaning against the cannon. Two of the king's lieutenants stood behind the cannon. Em-Pee thought he could identify one of them but was not sure because the picture was too grainy. Em-Pee suspected that if he had not fled from the Zulu Kingdom, he would have been one of those men. After all, he used to prepare the king's bath that he took on the iNkatha.

As it turned out, Farini's fortunes did not fall with Ulundi. Instead they rose. British audiences were even more eager to see the noble savages that had finally been subdued by the might of the British Empire after first disgracing the imperial forces at Isandlwana. For the rest of the year the performances went on, and the disgruntled Zulus continued to press for more money.

Finally they reached the end of their patience and went on strike. On Saturday, 3 January 1880, a standing-room-only house was waiting for the Zulus at the Aq, but they were nowhere to be seen. Various human curiosities had paraded, danced and exhibited themselves in their several forms of grotesquerie, but without the promised Zulus, the audience felt cheated. They started chanting for the Zulus. A livid Farini had to promise them a partial refund of the admission fees they had paid.

For weeks, the Zulus stood their ground. The Great Farini tried many tricks, even confiscating their clothes. The Zulus went to court with, Farini suspected, the assistance of liberal bleeding-hearts – particularly church people. He felt betrayed, for he had always treated his natives like his own family. He told the Justice of the Peace that he merely took their clothes to prevent them from wandering in the streets of London where they could be victims of crime.

Em-Pee, on the other hand, revealed that the Zulus had been offered more money by a rival impresario and Farini was trying to prevent them from selling their labour where it would be rewarded fairly.

'All we want is to be paid what we deserve for our work,' he said.

'I am willing to pay for their way back to Africa,' said Farini.

The newspapers had a field day with this strike, condemning the savages for ingratitude. Em-Pee read an article in *The Daily Telegraph* to his mates where the reporter was urging the police to 'arrest these wretched creatures immediately' for loitering, refusing to fulfil the terms of their contract with their employer, and living high on the hog on the police court's poor boxes. The

Zulus laughed out loud when Em-Pee got to the part where the newspaper said: *Meanwhile London is threatened by an impi of outrageous Zulus, determined to live here, but equally determined not to work.*

The Justice of the Peace advised the parties to work out an amicable solution. The Great Farini offered to decrease the number of performances and to improve their wages.

When the Zulus returned to work, many things had changed. Farini had imported new Zulus from France, and these included a Zulu princess called Amazulu. He billed them as Farini's Friendly Zulus. As an antithesis to Em-Pee's troupe of ferocious Zulus, the Parisian Zulus smiled a lot and only played games. Instead of threatening audiences with their assegais, they used the spears to compete with audience members at target aiming, and of course they hit the bullseye all the time. Unlike Em-Pee's Zulus, Farini's Friendly Zulus were said to be loyal to the British Crown.

Em-Pee suspected that Farini had introduced them to placate those who were trying to censor his human zoo. Noise was coming from various quarters, mostly the religious establishment, trying to shut Farini down.

Then P.T. Barnum saved the day by inviting The Great Farini and his human curiosities to join his ever-expanding big tent in New York. When Em-Pee showed reluctance to sail to yet another country, Farini convinced him that it was only a temporary move; it was important to export the Zulus to New York before Cetshwayo's shine wore off.

* * *

Between decks midway through the voyage is not the most pleasant place to be. Not only are the two toilets at each end of the deck exuding unpleasant odours, but the stench of unwashed bodies and decaying food and the fumes of rum permeate the area. It is not unbearable; the passengers have all become inured to it. They have no choice.

The Irishmen are beginning to thaw towards the Zulus, all thanks to Slaw, who shuttles between the groups, telling each side stories of heroism of the other. The Zulus have even performed some dances, which fascinated the ladies. They are more star-struck when they hear that Slaw and 'his' Zulus are going to join P.T. Barnum.

The men are jealous of the attention paid to the savages. They refer to the women as slags, which makes them angry and more defiant. Some women even lend the Zulus their pillows and blankets; Farini had not warned Em-Pee and his mates that you have to bring your own bedding in steerage. But the Zulus were managing all right, covering themselves with burlap sacks and rolling some up for pillows.

One woman who particularly fusses over the Zulus introduces herself as Aoife Murphy and declares, as soon as she hears they are prospective P.T. Barnum stars, that she has always wanted to join the circus. She can sing like a nightingale and dance like a prima ballerina. The Zulus teach her Zulu songs; she teaches them Irish songs.

Aoife Murphy stands in front of the Zulus as they sprawl on their straw mattresses and sings for them the Zulu lullaby *Thula, thula sana*. Occasionally she sips from a bottle of rum, makes faces, and holds it high above her head as she butchers the song. The Zulus don't seem to be paying much attention to her. They are either dozing off or having a soft conversation among themselves. An Irishman occasionally yells, 'Shut up, slut!'

Only Em-Pee is staring at her, goggle-eyed.

4

New York City – July 1885
The Dinka Princess

When Em-Pee sees her for the first time she is in a cage perched on a buckboard wagon. She wears a papier-mâché crown painted gold, and a patchwork cape of mink, otter and kodiak fur. The first thing that attracts him is her complexion. She is pitch black. Blacker than any night. Almost purple in her blackness. She is gangly, her legs twisted awkwardly to fit in the small cage. She squats uncomfortably, her head resting between her knees and her spindly arms wrapped tightly around them. Her fur coat covers her whole body and most of the floor of the cage, so that one is unable to say what dress or shoes she is wearing, if any.

He reads on a carved wooden cartouche attached to the cage that she is from the Dinka tribe in Sudan. She is called Dinkie the Dinka Princess, and is owned by Monsieur Duval, proprietor of Duval Ethnological Expositions.

He would have looked and moved on, but she smiles at him. Just vaguely. That is enough. He freezes and gazes at her. She averts her eyes slightly and once more the empty stare takes over.

He has been in Madison Square Park before, scouting for respectable performance venues outside the Tenderloin district, but has never seen the Dinka Princess. Only cages with pygmies, individual men and women or family units. Or some exotic creatures of the African and South American jungles – mandrills and drills, marmosets and moustached emperor tamarins, the latter in meshed-wire cages instead of behind iron bars. The Dinka Princess must be a new acquisition. Unless she has been transferred from a human zoo in another part of the city.

There are no pygmies today, so Dinkie is hogging all the attention. She is not doing anything, just sitting there with fiery red lips, thick and slightly pursed. Yet spectators are particularly engrossed in her, as if she is performing a hypnotic dance.

Their children are fascinated by the mandrills and other simians.

Men push Em-Pee to the side to get a better view of the caged woman. He is invisible. He is the only Black person in this crowd. The only one not in bondage. He tries to resist but the human tide is too powerful for him and soon he finds himself at the edge of the crowd. Nonetheless his steadfast gaze does not shift from the woman. Her gaze does not shift from the emptiness in the sky.

A few moments later, it does. Her eyes seem to be searching in the crowd and land on the spot where Em-Pee had previously been standing. They show some disappointment that he has been replaced by an old codger in an equally old British police visor cap. The eyes sweep the crowd once more, and brighten when they land on Em-Pee, meeting his and locking them in an unblinking stare. Em-Pee thinks he detects a smile. A slight one. Perhaps a suggestion of one. He smiles back. A really broad one. She smiles for real. Her teeth are blindingly white.

The heads of the spectators all turn to see what she is smiling at. They do not see Em-Pee. He is invisible. Instead, above his head, they see the exotic simians in their cages and the screeching children trying to provoke them to screech back. The spectators think that's what the caged woman is smiling at. How cute. They break into gentle laughter.

Em-Pee smiles even more broadly. The Dinka Princess stares at him curiously. Her brow and nose are glistening with perspiration. The July sun is merciless. She must be broiling in the small cage under such a heavy fur cape. But her nonchalance, broken only by vague smiles whenever her eyes drift to him, belies that.

He is attacked by sudden elation. It is a strange and fearful feeling. He walks slowly backwards while still gazing at the woman in the cage, until he is clear of the crowd, then he breaks into a run. He feels very bouncy all the way and is afraid that he may be getting sick. He does not return to Slaw and the troupe but goes straight to his tenement at Five Points.

'What's the matter, Em-Pee? Somebody's chasing you?' asks Aoife. He almost bumps into her and Mavo at the door. 'And you home so early?'

'Not feeling so good,' he says. 'You can leave Mavo. I am not going out tonight.'

This excites four-year-old Mavo. He goes to the circus with his mother every day, while his father is performing elsewhere, and enjoys being babysat by clowns, gymnasts, human curiosities and trapeze artists when his mother is performing. But staying home with his father for a change is a rare treat.

Aoife looks at Em-Pee suspiciously, shakes her head and leaves.

Soon Em-Pee regrets volunteering to look after the boy. He is much too active and won't let his father lie on the bed and rest. He wants a pillow fight, and the father fights back half-heartedly. He is still light-headed.

*　*　*

Mavo, named after an ancestor of the Mkhize clan, Mavovo, was conceived on the very first night Em-Pee landed in America almost five years ago.

When the steamship entered New York harbour, there was great excitement among the passengers, particularly the steerage folk, who would finally get some reprieve from the stuffy dungeon. Em-Pee's relief was that finally he and Aoife would go their separate ways, though, admittedly, he had grown fond of her. She had become quite enamoured of him as well, and took every opportunity to fuss over him. It was worse when she had had a few tots of rum. She planted herself next to him on the straw mattress and sang Zulu songs. The Zulus had taught her a few more in addition to the lullaby, and they were in stitches at her mispronunciation of the words.

But they had finally arrived at the Port of New York, and she was sure to go her way.

After Farini had settled with the collector of customs and the passengers had all gone through the Emigrant Landing Depot at Castle Garden in Battery Park, a process that took only a few hours, thanks to the help from P.T. Barnum's men who had come to meet the Zulus, Aoife told Em-Pee she was coming along. No one, not even Em-Pee, had seen this coming. She announced that she had made no arrangements for anyone to meet her, for she had no one, unlike the many steerage passengers who had excited relatives and friends meeting them.

'She's your problem, guv,' said Slaw with a naughty twinkle in his eye.

'I'm not a problem,' said Aoife. 'Just ask your boss to give me work.'

Farini did not wait to be asked. He turned and looked at her patronisingly. 'What can you do?' he asked.

'I can sing. Em-Pee's my witness.'

'Maybe you can, but we're not vaudeville,' said Farini dismissively and walked on.

'I can be an entertainer in many other ways,' said Aoife, skipping after him like a child.

'What I mean is, you don't have any deformity around which we can create a story. You're just a pretty lass, and that's not going to help anyone.'

Aoife stood her ground in front of The Great Farini and gestured at the Zulus.

'They don't have no deformity neither,' she said.

'They are Zulus,' said Farini, his expression showing his impatience at a woman who was so daft she could not see the obvious.

'I can be a Zulu too. I know how to sing Zulu songs.'

'As I said, young lady, I'm interested only in freaks and biological rarities. So is Mr Barnum, to whom I'm renting out these Zulus.'

Aoife was getting desperate. 'I can be a rarity too; I can be a freak.'

'Well, Em-Pee, as Slaw said, she's your problem,' said Farini.

She turned out to be a nice problem, after all. At a

boarding house booked for them for the night, Slaw was given his own room by the landlady as she found it inconceivable that he could sleep in the same room with 'the Negroes from Africa'. Aoife was allocated her own room as well. There would be no miscegenation under her roof. Em-Pee and the rest of the Zulus were all bunched together in one room.

Irrepressible Aoife, however, would not be separated from her Zulu warrior. In the middle of the night she smuggled him into her room. That night Mavovo was created. Well, he might have been conceived on subsequent nights at Five Points, where Farini found accommodation for the Zulus, but his parents liked to think of him as a Mulatto product of their first night in America.

Farini got Aoife a job with another impresario who ran the New York Museum of Biological Rarities. She was one of the unskilled musicians who were hired to sing discordant songs and make a terrible noise with trumpets and drums on the building's balcony to invite audiences in the manner Barnum's American Museum used to do until it burned to the ground in 1865.

If he could Em-Pee would have slaughtered a goat to thank his ancestors for placing him and Aoife on the same ship to America. And the White woman's ancestors for making her so forward and so shameless that she had insisted she was going with him – a thing that would never have been done by any woman in kwaZulu. He would never have ended up cohabiting with her if she had not taken the initiative. He was glad he allowed himself to be captured by her, despite the teasing and snide remarks of his fellow Zulus. She had smothered him with so much love that he forgot about Nomalanga and banished any desire to return to the old country to hunt her down and, married or not, to abduct her to some faraway land where no one would ever find them. He looked back at that yearning and chuckled at how silly and immature it was.

For three years they were as happy as any couple could be, despite their living conditions at a rookery. Though they did not walk together in the city, to avoid racial slurs, within the walls of their tenement the three of them shared a life of blissful oblivion.

But of late there has been tension in paradise. It started with Em-Pee's reversal of fortunes, and spousal disagreements on how to change that situation for the better. Moments of long silence are now followed by moments of loud squabbling and then followed once again by moments of long silence.

Aoife is even turned off by his breathing when they make love, something that takes him aback because she has never said that before in all their years of 'marriage'. She just lies there until he finishes his business. It never used to be like that. There was a time when she was so voracious she could eat him alive. Now she just lies there impassively.

When he asks, she says, 'It is your breathing. It disturbs me. It turns me off.'

'Should I face the other way when we make love?'

'No, I don't mean like that. Maybe you should just shut your mouth and not breathe through it.'

That's the ultimate, Em-Pee thinks. When she's annoyed by your breathing, that's a point of no return.

She sees the wounded look. She regrets blurting it out. She didn't mean to be unkind. It is not lost on her that lately she has been discovering many irritating things about him.

Their most glorious moments were the first few months in America. The Zulus were performing to great crowds in New York. Sometimes they would have a stint with P.T. Barnum at his big tent – performances in various cities, or they would be with William Coup, another impresario who was a close friend and business partner of Farini's, and who was famous for coming up with the concept of a circus train that travelled from city to city transporting performers and their materials.

When W.C. Coup's Circus travelled to such cities as Detroit and Chicago, Aoife and Mavo remained at Five Points because she had started the job singing discordantly at the New York Museum of Biological Rarities.

Em-Pee and the Zulus performed to crowds of up to twelve thousand in a tent with three rings – another one of Coup's inventions. Farini choreographed new Zulu war dances that were in keeping with American tastes. The Zulus still frightened the spectators; that was a Farini staple. What good were Zulus if they were not frightening people out of their wits? For instance, they ran into the circus ring screaming and yelling blue murder and hurling their assegais at predetermined targets that were frighteningly close to some spectators' faces. Or they demonstrated how they cut the throats of White people with their blunt assegais. Though no blood flowed, the demonstration looked so real that they left some in the crowds screaming.

Every night Slaw would be slaughtered to the orgasmic shrieks of spectators, and Em-Pee would be the chief slaughterer.

The Zulus engaged in other entertainments that were less gruesome. One event that Em-Pee relished, since it involved skill and prowess, was The Race of the Savage Races. Here, Americans Indians raced with the Zulus to the roar of the spectators. Sometimes he won the race; at other times an American Indian or another Zulu, perhaps Samson, won.

After the tours with the circus, he looked forward to returning to New York, to Five Points, to Aoife and Mavo. He vowed that one day he would take Mavo to kwa-Zulu, to perform the rituals that would welcome him into the clan, to introduce him to the ways of his people. Mavo needed to know his izithakazelo, clan praises, which would teach him about the origins of his people from the land of the blue lakes in Central Africa where abaMbo came from, right up to his great-grandfather, the great Zihlandlo, who was Shaka's ally and friend, but was assassinated by the troops of Dingane, Shaka's brother, on the hills of Nkandla. The boy could not navigate the world without the guidance of his ancestors, and it was sad that the ancestors did not even know of his existence. A proper introduction was essential, through the slaughter of a black bull and the brewing of sorghum beer. Most importantly, he needed to be properly integrated not only into the Mkhize clan but into the broader amaZulu nation, so that no affliction should befall him in the future.

A wave of sadness always assailed him whenever he thought of home. His people were no longer the people he left, standing tall and unvanquished. After Ulundi and the capture of his king, Cetshwayo kaMpande, in the Ngome Forest where he was hiding, kwaZulu was no longer an independent kingdom. After Cetshwayo's exile in Cape Town, he sailed to Britain to meet Queen Victoria to plead for the restoration of the kwaZulu Kingdom.

Em-Pee had just finished setting up the stage for the exhibit of Farini's Dwarf Earthmen, composed of his Kalahari Bushmen, at Steinway and Sons Hall, and was walking down the steps to 14th Street to catch a coach home, when Farini called him back.

'I've something for you, Em-Pee. Your king is in London.'

He showed him the *Illustrated London News*, 12 August 1882, with the headline 'Cetewayo in London'.

Farini read aloud, chuckling occasionally at the wonder of it all, how the king, travelling with a doctor, servants and an interpreter, and accompanied by a fleet of newspaper reporters, was greeted with cheers upon landing from *The Arab*, the ship that brought him from Cape Town. He was mobbed in the streets of London. The paper reported that he was 'a fine burly man with a pleasant, good-humoured face, though almost black; his manners are frank and jovial, but still dignified, and he wears a European dress'.

Farini laughed. This was not the savage king he imagined.

'Of course, he is a king; he would carry himself with dignity and composure, wouldn't he?' said Em-Pee, not hiding his annoyance.

Farini shook his head, and then read on: *In his demeanour Cetewayo is most gentle, utterly belying the popular conception which pictures him as a rude and turbulent savage. His intelligence is shown by the questions which he addresses to his interpreters, and his capacity to win men's friendship by the extraordinary sympathy felt with him by the passengers of* The Arab. *He has been, in fact, everyone's friend, and the passengers who left the ship at Plymouth bade him a hearty farewell.*

Every day Em-Pee keenly followed Cetshwayo's so-journ in London from dispatches that came from Eng-land. He had lengthy discussions with Farini about the situation in kwaZulu.

Farini's biggest regret was that Cetshwayo's British visit happened when his shows had migrated to New York. Otherwise he would have featured the Zulu king in them.

'After all, you knew him personally, guv,' Slaw added. 'You would have asked him to be on display with our Zulus.'

'If Cetewayo came to America our business would boom again,' added Farini.

Spectators would finally set their eyes on the savage king who had slain hundreds of British soldiers. Farini said he read that the king was still a celebrity in England and thousands came to see him whenever he appeared. But these were not paying spectators, which was a waste of a good opportunity.

'I would not have allowed that,' said Em-Pee emphat-ically. 'I won't be party to any situation where my king is insulted.'

'Insulted, old chap? Do you feel insulted when you educate Americans about your people and your culture?' asked Farini, looking rather wounded.

'You're just joking, guv, aren't you?' said Slaw. 'You're just saying it because you know we can't get the old bugger to come to New York to join our shows?'

'He is my king, damn you! He is the king of amaZulu people!'

In subsequent weeks Farini and Em-Pee read about how the British queen granted Cetshwayo his wish and allowed him to return to kwaZulu. He had spent about ten months in London, and his celebrity grew throughout the time he was there.

When he returned to kwaZulu, he found that his kingdom had shrunk tremendously, what with colonist farmers encroaching more and more into his territory, and big chunks allocated by the Natal colonist government to those amaZulu people who declared they no longer wanted him as king!

In any event, kwaZulu was no longer a free and independent country. It had now been annexed to the British Empire, and Cetshwayo had become a mere paramount chief, a vassal of Queen Victoria. According to Em-Pee, even his second crowning, by Sir Theophilus Shepstone on 29 January 1883, was merely symbolic. His crown came with emasculated power.

Em-Pee felt it was a merciful end when a civil war erupted and forced Cetshwayo to escape to the town of Eshowe, where he died only a year after his return to the meaningless throne.

Cetshwayo's death affected both Em-Pee and Farini for different reasons. Em-Pee mourned the glorious days when he'd served the king, even bathing him, and caroused with isigodlo girls. Nostalgia assailed him and he became morose. This contributed to the tensions in the house.

Farini, on the other hand, mourned the loss of business because he believed that Cetshwayo's celebrity would wane after his demise. Gradually, the glory of Isandlwana would diminish in the imagination of the spectators and soon he would have to conceive new fascinations that would sustain the relevance of the Zulus.

While Farini agonised over these issues, Em-Pee was brooding over John Dunn's treachery. The White man who had been pampered by the king and had married more than forty Zulu wives, including princesses from the royal house, had turned against his benefactor and pledged loyalty to the British. In return, he was given tracts of lands as a buffer between Natal and kwaZulu.

'It shows you can never trust the White man,' said Em-Pee.

'Except if that White man is me,' said The Great Farini, smiling. 'I have given you and your Zulus a good life away from the savage wars of your tribes.'

'I'm sure you believe it's a good life,' said Em-Pee.

Em-Pee said it as if it was a joke, but Farini suspected that he was becoming disgruntled again and would influence the other Zulus to adopt the same attitude. He still harboured a grudge against Em-Pee as the instigator of the strike in London. He blamed himself for ever renting out the Zulus to P.T. Barnum, who was reputed to pay his performers such exorbitant wages that many of them became wealthy in their own right.

Farini had cursed out loud when he heard how much P.T. was paying his Zulus. 'How do you think I'm going to afford them when they finish the stint with you?' he had asked.

And indeed, there were plenty of murmurs when the Zulus returned to their meagre wages. Em-Pee told his mates, 'I shouldn't have come back. I should have stayed in Canada.'

He was referring to an incident in Detroit when he had become so fed up with the Camel Man that he absconded for days. The Camel Man had insisted he clean up the dung after a camel had an accident in one of the rings. Em-Pee told him he had nothing to do with circus animals; he was himself a performer. When the quarrel almost turned to blows, the management took the Camel Man's side. Em-Pee walked away from the big tent and crossed the bridge into Canada.

The circus managers thought it was just a temporary Zulu tantrum and that he would soon return. When he didn't, they sent out a search party, which discovered him having a wonderful time at a tavern in Windsor. He meekly returned to Detroit with them, and to the big tent. The fear of deserting his family, especially of never seeing Mavo again, brought him back to his senses.

Two of his Zulu mates did finally leave, after getting a more attractive offer from a rival impresario. Farini did not fancy another sea voyage to southern Africa to acquire a whole new bunch of Zulus. He recruited Negroes, auditioned them and selected some for his act. It was Em-Pee's task to teach them how to be Zulus.

It was not unusual to have American Negroes assume Zulu identities. Thanks to Cetshwayo, Zulus were so fashionable that there were street performers all over New York who passed for Zulu. Indeed, some copycat impresarios had added Zulus to their repertoires, most of whom were Americans. The whole of New York and its environs was overrun by Zulus who were screaming like wild men, dancing crazy dances and threatening spectators with badly made assegais and painted timber shields.

It was precisely because of these faux Zulus that the impresario had billed himself as The Great Farini and his Genuine Zulus. This billing did not change with the introduction of Negroes. After all, they were taught Zuluness by a genuine Zulu.

Now that he had more recruits – both male and fe-male – he had to allocate quite a few of them to other tribes of Africa. Using a book by John George Wood, *Illustrated History of the Uncivilized Races*, he assigned the Negro recruits to various tribes. Some became Maasai tribesmen from East Africa, others BaKongo from Central Africa. It did not matter that he did not have anyone to assist him in training the Negroes to be true to their new identities. He read about the customs of various groups and improvised the rest.

The Great Farini peppered his lectures before the exhibits or performances with Darwinian theory that was half-baked to the erudite but appeared wise and deep to the less schooled.

The first appearance of the revamped show was at Madison Square Garden, a venue with which Em-Pee was familiar since he had appeared there in his very first year in America with the P.T. Barnum circus.

In his lecture, The Great Farini first dismissed rumours that among his performers, passing as genuine Zulus, were Irish immigrants 'cunningly painted and made up to look like savages'. When he said this, Em-Pee covertly pinched Slaw, who was in the wings with him and the other Zulus, painted brown and ready to battle with the Zulus as a savage from some unnamed Indian Ocean islands.

As usual the show was well received. Spectators loved The Battle of the Savage Tribes where the Zulus fought against the Maasai, and the Maasai fought against the BaKongo. They raised the roof with cheers when a tiny savage David, also known as Slaw by his mates, felled a giant Zulu Goliath, a certain Mpiyezintombi, and when wild Zulus performed their wild dance and demonstrated how they slaughtered White men, and when

BaKongo demonstrated how they cooked White missionaries in a giant three-legged pot.

That was Em-Pee's last show with Farini. He resigned summarily. A few days later the other Zulus, Samson and the mates he came with from Cape Town, left Farini's stable as well.

Slaw felt out of place without the Zulus. He left The Great Farini to join them.

* * *

Em-Pee is back at Madison Square Park, standing below the cage. The Dinka Princess is watching him disapprovingly. Since he discovered her, he has been coming every day and gazing silently at her. For hours. She gazes back unflinchingly, as if in a dare. Sometimes she gets tired of the sight of him and transfers her gaze to some spot in the sky. Always the same spot. She stares at it so intently that the spectators are tempted to look up, hoping to see whatever it is that she sees. Her eyes return to him after a while, and glare into his eyes. Sometimes her eyes search, sweeping over the heads of the spectators – he doesn't stand at the same spot every day – until they find him. Her eyes light up in a eureka spark, with the whites becoming whiter and the brown irises becoming shimmering black.

His work has suffered because of frequenting this

cage to bathe his battered soul in her presence. His colleagues do not understand what is happening to him. Their business is suffering; instead of attending to it, he stands mesmerised by a woman in a cage. He has even missed some performances as a result.

When the Zulus rebelled and broke out of Farini's chains, they formed their own group, which aimed to create a professional environment free of competition and hierarchy. They named themselves the Genu-Wine Zulus to indirectly trash The Great Farini and his Genuine Zulus, and also the shameless outfits proliferating on the streets of New York passing for Zulus and performing silly jigs. They were all equal owners of the company and decided everything by consensus, since none of them had a managerial position.

But soon the White member of the group found himself taking the lead in negotiating deals because the White promoters and impresarios would talk only to a fellow White. By the time the group woke up to the fact, Slaw was the dealmaker and decision maker. He was regarded as the master and the Zulus as the servants.

He often forgot and carried himself like a master. Only Em-Pee called him to order occasionally and reminded him of his true station.

Whereas Slaw spends most of the time dealing with administrative issues, Em-Pee's creative decisions usually carry the day. For instance, the Genu-Wine Zulus distinguish themselves from all the other Zulus of New York by their performances, which are based on authentic Zulu dances such as isishameni from the Msinga area of kwaZulu, isizingili from the southern coastal areas, and khwenxa from uKhahlamba region. All these dances are graceful to watch and have a deep cultural meaning, especially to Em-Pee, who used to be much admired by the maidens for being a nimble dancer. The dancers perform in unison in formations, with rhythmic foot-stomping to the song they sing themselves. Occasionally a dancer breaks out into a solo, kicking his legs up high and then throwing himself to the ground. The performers try very hard to be different from the deadly Zulus of Farini's creation. They smile a lot, and exchange friendly banter with spectators, led by Slaw, who passes for an impresario.

Their greatest difficulty is in booking venues. They perform often at the small clubs in the Tenderloin, competing with blackface banjo-strumming White men passing for Zulu, and with strippers, revues and sundry vaudeville acts. When they have failed to hire a venue or to be hired by a club, they busk in the street. Em-Pee's dream is that one day they will hit the big time and perform at Madison Square Garden.

But Slaw is not a skilled impresario and does not know how to negotiate with promoters and venue owners. Often, they don't take him seriously; he is puny and not that well groomed. He has taken to wearing a bowler hat and smoking a cigar to look more important. His accent helps him with those Americans who associate British accents with class and erudition but betrays him to those who are well travelled and notice that it is peppered with too much street argot.

When Em-Pee is sent by his mates to scout for venues, he goes to admire the Dinka Princess instead. Work suffers. His mates are worried about him, though none of them is aware of his new pastime.

Recently a stroke of luck took the Genu-Wine Zulus to a performance venue in Hartford, Connecticut. They were away for eight days, and Em-Pee couldn't visit the Dinka Princess for that long. Hence her disapproving gaze today. He is certain he is not imagining it. In fact, it is not just a disapproving gaze that welcomes him when he stands in front of the cage after elbowing his way confidently through the crowd with a lot of 'excuse me's, pretending to be a labourer who has something to do at the cage. He sees a flash of anger in her eyes, accompanied by a twitch of her lips. He shapes his mouth into 'I'm sorry'. He has no idea what he is sorry about.

Her eyes become softer and playful. Then they become glassy with unshed tears. His become glassy too, but he is unable to imprison the tears in his eyes. They drop down his cheeks one by one. He is embarrassed. He tries to hide his face as he rubs them away with the back of his hand. She breaks into a smile. And a tiny tinny giggle. The spectators have never seen this before. They have never heard a single sound uttered from her lips. They all sigh in unison and exclaim, 'Aah!' Their heads turn from side to side, attempting to see what could have caused this unheard-of occurrence. None of them can see Em-Pee. He is invisible. So are his tears.

He is ashamed of himself. He is also angry with her for making him cry in public. He pushes his way out of the crowd and runs out of the park and down Broadway into the inner Tenderloin. He catches a coach to the Black Bull, an English pub on the Bowery.

Slaw is at the bar, puffing on a cigar.

'Maybe we should just give this up, guv, and go back to Farini,' says Slaw before Em-Pee even pulls up a stool.

'He said we burned our bridges when we left him,' says Em-Pee.

'We can beg him to take us back. I know how to beg.'

'Yeah, you mastered that on the streets of London. But I'm no beggar. I am a Zulu, son of Mavovo. I haven't come to America to beg anyone.'

'But your heart is no longer on this, guv,' says Slaw.

'If you got us good venues my heart would be in it.'

'If you stopped all this nonsense of friendly Zulus we would be popular again. We used to make a lot of money when you guys were savages. All of a sudden you're too hoity-toity to be a savage.'

This kind of debate has become heated lately, with the other members of the troupe supporting Slaw's view that the Genu-Wine Zulus will only reclaim their glory if they perform dances that are menacing. As they did when they were with The Great Farini, who was not called great for nothing, they should demonstrate how they slaughtered White men at Isandlwana and curdle the spectators' blood by pretending to attack them with assegais. The orderly dances that are beautifully choreographed and reflect the true culture of the Zulus do not put bread on the table. Americans want to see savages, not some namby-pamby Zulus who are all smiles and kiss babies.

'Remember Farini's Friendly Zulus?' asks Em-Pee. 'They worked in London, they can work here too.'

'They worked only for a while, but people lost interest in them. People want blood. Horror is the thing these days.'

'Vaudeville is doing great, yet they don't frighten anybody. Instead they make their audiences laugh. We can do the same; we can create joy and laughter.'

'You're Zulus, not vaudeville. In vaudeville, audiences laugh with the comedians. Who wants to laugh with the Zulus? Folks would rather laugh at you, not with you. That's what pays the bills.'

The argument always goes back to Davis. Almost two years ago the Genu-Wine Zulus had sent Em-Pee to watch The Wild Zulu presented at Longacre Square by the impresario Davis. The hope was that the Genu-Wine Zulus would get a few lessons on how to make their show as popular as Davis. Staged outdoors, without paying exorbitant venue fees, his shows were garnering even upper-crust audiences who otherwise would be in concert halls and opera houses. Slaw had consulted Davis who, for a small fee, had agreed to give them a few tips on how to change the focus of their dwindling business into a going concern.

However, after watching The Wild Zulu eat raw meat and perform savagery in the most disgusting manner, Em-Pee put his foot down that the Genu-Wine Zulus would keep to their authentic Zuluness.

Things are getting worse for the Genu-Wine Zulus. Perhaps Em-Pee will now change his mind and do the sensible thing, thinks Slaw.

'I think we should go back to Davis,' says Slaw.

'I'm not going to eat raw meat,' says Em-Pee. 'None of my people will. You can eat raw meat, Slaw, if you have the taste for it.'

'But I'm not a Zulu, Em-Pee, otherwise I would eat it. We must follow Davis's advice if we want to survive. Maybe even go for a partnership with him. He told us Americans ain't no pussies. They want action. Maybe we can think of some interesting savage action, even if it's not eating raw meat.'

This quarrel follows Em-Pee home. This time with Aoife, who has become increasingly impatient with him. Em-Pee is not bringing home much money; they have to survive on what she earns from her discordant singing stints, which are now becoming old with the audiences and the calls are few and far between.

'I must present my people with dignity,' he tells Aoife.

'We cannot eat dignity,' she says.

The following week Aoife runs away with the circus, doing minstrelsy singing of what she claims are Zulu songs and some clowning for the kids.

Em-Pee is stuck with Mavo. He toys with the idea of finding his way back home. But what is he going to do with a kid who looks so white in kwaZulu? He recalls that there were kids like that in his country. Mavo would not be out of place. John Dunn had made numerous Mulatto kids with his Zulu wives.

5

New York City – December 1886
The Snow Princess

Snow piles up on the sidewalks and pavements as Em-Pee trudges towards Madison Square Park. His boots leave a trail of prints that quickly fill up. She will not be there; he knows that already. It would be foolish of him to expect her to be there in this kind of weather. Though owners of human curiosities are a greedy lot, they would not be so inhuman as to expose their meal tickets to such inclement conditions. They would not even expect paying customers to brave the cold just to ogle a pygmy or a Dinka woman. Except, perhaps, the White men in stylish suits who he has observed masturbating covertly under their broad capes to this hapless caged woman. Even under the patchwork of furs that she wears in even the hottest of summers, she would be frostbitten to death today.

He knows all this, yet he goes. He needs his fix. Just to gaze at her. Or at the spot where the wagon with her cage would have been parked. Unlike the masturbating men, there is nothing perverse in his obsession. Just a gaze and he will be satisfied. He has been coming to Madison Square Park for the past seventeen months just for the gaze. He has never thought of her in any sexual manner. He wonders if he even sees her as a woman. Maybe as a child. Or just a marvel.

Of course, she is not there. No cages of human curiosities, no men and women leering, no exotic creatures of South American jungles, no dog-walkers. Only trees, shrubs and benches dressed in the white that has transformed them into phenomenal monsters.

He is not disappointed. At least he tried. One day she will know that he made an effort to see her even when he knew she would not be there. The attempt itself is satisfaction enough. Hopefully it will be satisfaction to her too, when she gets to know of it. Perhaps she knows already. She has this habit of scrutinising him with an all-knowing eye whenever he comes after an absence of a few days. As if she is saying, I know where you've been; I was there with you in spirit.

He must return home before it gets dark. Must arrive there before Mavo. He gave him permission to shovel snow in the neighbourhood for a few coins. He worries about Mavo. If Em-Pee had already performed amasiko rituals to fortify him for the world out there, he wouldn't be so perturbed.

Em-Pee is obsessed with the idea of taking Mavo to the old country – that's what he calls kwaZulu, after the Irish circus folk who call Ireland that – to introduce him to the ancestors. He does not know when that will be or how it will be achieved. In the meantime, he teaches him all he knows about reading and writing, and about the story of his people. He is wary of sending him to the Five Points Mission, an institution that provides aid to the destitute, holds literacy classes for their children, and attempts to convert the stubborn Irish Catholics to Methodism on Sundays. Or back to the Five Points House of Industry, just across from the mission, where he had been a pupil until he absconded.

Em-Pee used to take Mavo to the House of Industry in the morning, go to gaze at the Dinka Princess, and then pick him up in the afternoon. Sometimes, on the few occasions Em-Pee was performing with the Friendly Zulus, Mavo would be the only child waiting on the steps of the mission building long after the others had gone home. Each day Em-Pee was torn between his parental duties as a single father, his commitment to gazing at the Dinka Princess, and his obligations to the Friendly Zulus.

He had finally managed to convince his partners to call the troupe that instead of the Genu-Wine Zulus. Slaw and the other partners had resisted because friendliness was not paying the bills, and the name was clearly stolen from The Great Farini. Em-Pee stood his ground;

The Great Farini did not own the name and had no copyright on it. He, on the other hand, was an authentic Zulu who was also very friendly, as all the troupe members could vouch, and was more entitled to the name than a White man from Canada. It also helped that some folks laughed at the name Genu-Wine Zulus. It was a fake name, they said, reflecting the fakeness of the performers.

'Ain't nothing genuine about Genu-Wine Zulus,' prospective spectators said.

Darkness had already fallen one day when he arrived at the House of Industry, and Mavo was nowhere to be seen. Em-Pee hoped he was in the building with the children who were resident there and were being taken care of by the institution. But the caretakers had last seen him when he came to eat his meal of bread and gruel, and then left to wait outside for his father.

Em-Pee prayed that Aoife, wherever she was travelling in the circus train, would not discover that he had lost their son. He searched the streets and alleys of Five Points every day, enquiring of hoboes and homeless kids if they had seen Mavo. They had, of course, seen many Mavos and would not have had any idea which one was his. The streets of Five Points were littered with Mavos.

Nevertheless, he continued to visit Madison Square Park to gaze at the woman in a cage.

After two weeks, he heard from women neighbours who knew Aoife that Mavo had been seen with a group of Street Arabs hawking newspapers on one occasion, and blacking shoes at Park Row on another. Em-Pee went there but did not find him. He did not give up. He spent hours gazing at the woman by day, and searching alleys known to be frequented by Street Arabs by night. Once he was chased by the New York Metropolitan Police, who suspected he was a mischief-maker.

A few days later two men from the Children's Aid Society came knocking at Em-Pee's tenement, one of them holding Mavo by the scruff of the neck as if he were a criminal. He had been spending his nights at a home for orphan newsboys and bootblacks run by the society. They took care of him, thinking he was an orphan or a homeless kid like the rest. It was only recently that he told them he had a father and a mother right there at Five Points. They did not believe him, but took a chance and brought him in case he was telling the truth.

'You done beat up this boy,' said one of them. 'He told us his dad is a Zulu.'

'No, I did no such thing,' said Em-Pee. 'I am a working man and went to fetch him at the House of Industry but he was gone.'

'Your papa works so hard for you and you run with Street Arabs?'

'He hates me,' screamed Mavo. 'My mama hates me too. She left me with him, and he don't care nothing and is gone all day long.'

This, to Em-Pee, was like an assegai ripping his diaphragm. But he is a Zulu warrior. He must pretend to be unscathed by tenderness.

'You're a Zulu man, all of six years old. You must be tough,' said Em-Pee. He turned to the men. 'I must work. He can't run away with Street Arabs every time I am late picking him up. He must be tough. In the old country, boys his age look after goats already.'

'This ain't no old country,' said one of the men. 'Ain't no goats here. Only pigs roaming the streets.'

'Your papa has to work for you, boy,' said the second man. 'You lucky you have a papa who works himself to the bone for you.'

'I work for myself,' said Mavo, taking some coins from his pocket and showing them to the men. 'I don't need nobody to work for me. I work for myself.'

The man advised Em-Pee to arrange with one of the lodging houses run by the Children's Aid Society to look after Mavo when he was working. There he would get a warm meal and a warm bed and would be taught a trade to boot.

* * *

Snow has stopped falling, but Em-Pee does not bother brushing off the pile on his cap and frock coat. He stands by the entrance to the park for a while, debating whether or not he should take a horsecar. They may or may not allow him inside, depending on the kindness of the conductor. In this kind of weather, he is not inclined to ride on the exterior platform at the rear of the car or upfront with the horses.

The mood of some of those conductors who allowed Black folk inside the car, provided there was no objection from the White passengers, has changed so much lately – ever since newspapers have been publishing horror stories of uppity Negroes who are talking of equality. Worse still, when they hear his voice they know immediately he is a foreigner.

They always ask, 'You have an accent, where are you from?' When he tells them he is a Zulu, an authentic one, some turn their noses the other way. To many White folk, Zulus are no longer the heroes they used to be, thanks to Black and White American charlatans who populate the streets in the guise of Zulus.

Even the *New York Times* recently complained of the wild behaviour of Arab, Turkish and Zulu performers who were accused of commandeering a train on their way to a fair in Chicago after some dispute with their impresario. The paper accused the business people who brought these natives of 'picking up in Cairo, Constantinople and Cape Town the cheapest and dirtiest Arabs, Turks and Zulus they could find'. Although these events happened in Illinois, some White New Yorkers look at these foreigners with suspicion and would be wary of sitting next to one in a streetcar.

He walks slowly on a recently shovelled sidewalk past the rows of brownstone mansions of the upper-crust Manhattanites in the Madison Square Park neighbourhood. His thoughts have drifted to the business. He wonders if Slaw and the other partners will agree to relocate to another city, since Zulus are losing their shine in New York. The Midwest may be thrilled by the graceful dance of a different breed of Zulus – the Friendly Zulus. There are many county and state fairs that would be enriched culturally by their performances.

And there she is, sitting in the middle of a flight of steps leading to the ornate door of a brownstone mansion. At first he thinks she is an apparition. But as he walks closer he decides she cannot but be real. She holds a black and brown box that he cannot make out and is looking intently into it. She raises her head, and as soon as she sees him she points the box at him. He is confused for a while and just stands there staring at her. She is peering at the box. He walks towards the stairs.

'Don't move,' she yells.

It is the first time he hears her voice. It is full-bodied and thick, commanding and forceful. He stops right there. She tries to be very steady with the box that is resting on her knee, but her hands are shaking a bit. She stands up, and he notices how tall she really is. Her head would touch the top of his door frame if she were to stand there. She makes to walk towards the door of the mansion.

He calls after her, 'Hey!'

She stops and looks down at him. Her pitch-blackness shimmers against the whiteness of the snow. Over a flowing white dress that blends with the snow she wears a red cape. He dares not climb the steps towards her.

Em-Pee smiles and says, 'Oh, so they do let you out of your cage sometimes?'

'Of course they do,' she says. 'It would be inhuman to keep me there all the time, forever and ever, amen.'

'You're a church girl then? I've only heard those words in church.'

'You go to church?'

'Only when my wife forces me to.'

'You even have a wife?'

'Don't change the subject. I asked about you first. You and church.'

'Been there occasionally when my master forces me to go. He says he wants to cleanse the false heathen gods out of me so that I know Jesus died for my sins.'

'What sins did you commit then?'

She giggles. She obviously doesn't understand what sinning entails. He has some idea, albeit a vague one. His Catholic wife used to drum it into his head, especially during the final months when their marriage was falling apart due to his insistence on dignity. Whereas church never mattered before, even for her, now she insisted that he and Mavo go and pray for their sins. She wailed that they were suffering because she had married a heathen man from darkest Africa who knew nothing about the Saviour, and that repentance was essential in all their lives.

Since she took the circus train, Em-Pee had never bothered to be saved again.

'So, are you going to tell me or not?' he asks, chuckling.

Instead of responding, she climbs the few steps to the door and opens it. Before she walks into the house she takes a long curious look at him. She bangs the door shut.

He stands there for a while, hoping the door will open again. It doesn't.

6

New York City – June 1887
The Photograph

The New York Giants have beaten the Philadelphia Phillies 29–1 and the streets are drunk with euphoria. As the crowds spill out of the Polo Grounds, Em-Pee and Slaw wait outside a 110th Street refreshment station. They have been waiting for a while, as the game took longer than expected.

Em-Pee is impatient; he'd rather be at Madison Square Park. Just to make sure one more time. After last winter, Dinkie the Dinka Princess did not return to the park. Early in spring he had gone there to fulfil his yearning. She was not there. Nor were the other displays. Instead, the whole place was fenced in and boarded up, as if being prepared for construction work. He went again after a few days; the same situation obtained. Perhaps today, whatever improvements were being done have been completed and the displays are back.

'Do you trust this man?' asks Em-Pee. 'What makes you think he'll keep his word?'

'Why wouldn't he?' asks Slaw. 'He's a sharp impresario;

there's something in it for him too. If anyone can pull off this deal, it's Davis.'

Sports fans are a predictable lot. They lose the game, they are so angry they vandalise everything and beat up one or two Negroes for the heck of it. They win the game, they are so happy they vandalise everything and beat up one or two Negroes for the heck of it. Some of them look at Em-Pee with beady eyes as they pass. But Slaw's presence saves the day. He is not just a loitering Negro; he is with his master.

Slaw puffs on his cigar pompously, as befitting the hotshot impresario he imagines he is. After a while they can see Davis limping along with a cane.

'We'll walk,' he says, without so much as a greeting. He's a man of little ceremony. 'It's only half an hour from here.'

'Are you going to be all right though?' asks Slaw.

'I'm not an invalid. Just a small sprain. Fell down the stairs.'

As they walk along, Davis says that even before they discuss anything else they must agree that he will get a fifty per cent cut on any deal that they make.

'Of course,' says Slaw. 'It's only fair, since you're introducing us to these guys.'

'I don't think so,' says Em-Pee. 'I, for one, want to know first what this deal is all about and what's in it for us.'

Davis looks at him disdainfully. 'Is this not the fella I allowed to see The Wild Zulu for free and he decided he was too hoity-toity for that kind of performance?'

'I just didn't have the appetite for raw meat,' says Em-Pee.

'He's going to be the death of you in this business, Slaw. Watch him.'

'This is different, man,' says Slaw. 'It's not like The Wild Zulu.'

'The Wild Zulu makes more money than you'll ever dream of,' says Davis. 'But, yes, this is different. This is theatre. This is Broadway.'

He tells them about Niblo's Garden on Broadway and Prince Street, which will be producing a musical play titled *She* based on a story by Henry Rider Haggard. It is a very exciting story, Davis explains, that Em-Pee and his Zulus will love tremendously, as it features their people. It is about a journey of two Englishmen, Horace Holly and Leo Vincey, their servant Job, and the Arab captain of their wrecked ship, Mahomed, into the hinterland of Africa. They are captured by a tribe of savages known as Amahagger, who cook the hapless Mahomed for dinner. The adventurers discover that the tribe is ruled by a White woman, a queen known as She, or She-Who-Must-Be-Obeyed, who is ferocious and fearsome. The rest of the story is compelling and intriguing, and they can read it for themselves if they are interested. The book is available at Brentano's or any other popular bookstore in New York.

'I have talked with the producer about my idea of having the savages in the play played by your real Zulus, Slaw,' says Davis, beaming at the brightness of the idea.

Slaw beams as well. It is indeed a bright idea.

The front-of-house manager leads them to the producer's office. Even before the three men take their seats, Skildore Skolnik, the producer, tells them there is no deal.

'But you promised,' says Davis. He is much more exasperated than his two companions, who are used to rejection.

'I didn't promise you a deal. I promised to talk to the director about it. He rejects the idea, and I share his view. Niblo's is a real theatre, not a gimmick or a human circus.'

'This is reputed to be the venue where P.T. Barnum had his first show ever,' says Davis indignantly. 'You can't get more human circus than Barnum.'

'That was fifty years ago,' says Skolnik. 'Niblo's is a respectable Broadway theatre now. We employ real actors here, not freaks.'

Em-Pee is curious about what it takes to be a real actor rather than a human curiosity. After all, in their performances they are acting all the time. When they scream and shout and pretend to slit a White man's throat with their assegais, it is all make-believe. It is not who they are in their real lives. Isn't that what acting is about?

'I am an actor. A real actor,' says Em-Pee.

'You can audition if you think you have what it takes,' says Skolnik. 'I can arrange that. If the director likes your acting he will give you a role, not because you are a genuine savage but because you are a good actor.'

Em-Pee likes the sound of this. He offers to audition.

'You're just thinking of yourself and not the troupe, Em-Pee,' says Slaw.

'Yep,' says Davis. 'If they take him as an actor, that's the end of the Friendly Zulus.'

As they are ushered out of Niblo's, Em-Pee says he has changed his mind about auditioning. Instead he has a better idea. They look at him, puzzled.

'Isandlwana!' he screams.

Although King Cetshwayo died three years ago, and a lot of his popularity is diminishing because people have short memories, a musical play about the Battle of Isandlwana, performed by the Friendly Zulus and a few other professional actors, could garner good audiences.

Em-Pee offers to sit down with Davis, and together they can work on a proposal that Davis will submit to Skildore Skolnik at Niblo's Garden.

* * *

Now that Mavo is resident at one of the lodging houses run by the Children's Aid Society, where they feed him at least two meals a day, train him in a trade, and preach to him about the bounties in heaven that are awaiting those who have handed their lives over to Jesus, Em-Pee has regained his freedom. He can come and go as he pleases and spends very little time at his Mulberry Bend tenement.

Occasionally the Friendly Zulus busk on some Lower Manhattan sidewalk and collect a few coins for sustenance, or on a lucky week get a real gig at some club on Church, Thompson or Sullivan streets, an area known as Black Broadway. The troupe has been depleted, many of its members having drifted to other outfits of performing Zulus or been swallowed by taverns and opium dens. The only one who continues to be loyal and is available to join Em-Pee and Slaw whenever they ask is Samson, who also works as a security guard at a neighbourhood bordello in Five Points.

The busking, therefore, is reduced to a three-man performance of genuine Zulu dances, the third man being Slaw, who has no choice but to dance as a White man who was brought up by a Zulu woman after being abandoned by his parents in a forest during what is vaguely termed the Anglo-Zulu War. Slaw's new biography has sparked interest and his inclusion in the dance as a White Zulu has made the performances more palatable for some spectators. He has lent credibility to the concept of friendly Zulus. The Friendly Zulus are so friendly that they adopted a White man as a brother instead of eating him. Or whiteness, courtesy of the White Zulu, has tamed the rest of the Zulus to the extent that their dances are rhythmic and beautiful instead of the wild, disorderly and brutal screams and gyrations expected of Zulu savages. The whiteness has also uncreased their faces from deadly frowns to gentle smiles.

On some days, Davis comes to Em-Pee's tenement to work on the proposal for *The Battle of Isandlwana*, the musical that they want to stage at Niblo's Garden. Davis has already spoken to Skildore Skolnik about it, and the producer thinks that if it is well packaged and strongly motivated he can sell the idea to investors.

Em-Pee had offered to join Davis at his brownstone mansion on Madison Avenue, but Davis insisted that he'd rather work with Em-Pee at his Five Points tenement. Em-Pee did not understand why a great impresario like Davis would want to work at a rookery in a stuffy room with makeshift furniture instead of an airy study surrounded by books at his mansion. He nevertheless understood when Davis explained that he thought Em-Pee's imagination would be more productive in familiar surroundings. The luxury of his mansion would overwhelm him and stunt his creativity.

The sessions with Davis are playful and full of laughter. He listens to Em-Pee's stories of beautiful Zulu maidens and courtship rituals with fascination, and bursts out laughing at the saucy parts. He says stories of maidens are essential; even though the story is about kings and soldiers and war, for it to be attractive to the audience there must be a love story. There must be beautiful maidens who will dance bare-breasted as he has seen in the displays of human curiosities at some of the venues in New York City.

After one of these sessions, the two men stroll together out of Mulberry Bend, Davis still talking excitedly about the Zulu maidens and Em-Pee digesting his doubts at what threatens to be a corruption of the story of his king and his people. Usually it takes Em-Pee forty minutes at most to walk from Five Points to Madison Square Park, but it might take them all of one hour today because of Davis's limp. It is much better than it was when they met the other day, but the pain is noticeable on his face every time he steps on to a higher or lower plane. Steadily they walk on Broadway, with Davis doing most of the talking.

On Madison Avenue they part ways. Davis walks into one of the brownstone mansions and Em-Pee goes on to his haunt at Madison Square Park, using the 23rd Street entrance, which is closer to the area where all the action used to be concentrated. The landscapers of the

New York Park Commission are done with revamping the park, and it has been cleared of all the displays and human curiosity exhibits. The spectators and the vendors have been replaced by lush lawns, neat rows of trees, flowers and dog-walkers.

His homing instinct takes him to where the wagon with a cage used to be parked. It is still there, but only in his mind. Vague and fuzzy. She is like a wide-eyed ghost in the mist. If ghosts came in purple. He tries to summon a clearer image of her. She obliges, not as Dinkie the Dinka Princess in a golden papier-mâché crown and a patchwork of furs, but as the purple Snow Princess of six months ago. He sits on a bench, closes his eyes and savours the image. It is not enduring. Soon it fades as he sinks into sleep.

He is awoken by galloping hooves, grinding wheels and the boisterous hollers of men. He can see, on 23rd Street, a New York City Police patrol wagon drawn by two well-fed horses and loaded with nine policemen, including the driver, in full uniform. He hides behind a nearby bush for fear that they might pick him up for loitering. They did that only three days ago when he was indeed loitering outside the Madison Avenue brownstone mansion where he had last seen the Dinka Princess. Apparently someone called the police after seeing him walking repeatedly up and down the street, stopping in front of the house, looking at the door fixedly, and then walking on, only to return after a few moments. Property owners could not be blamed if they thought he was casing the houses for future burglaries.

The police hauled him to the precinct. It took many hours of interrogation and explaining that he was a performing Zulu who was down on his luck and looking for employment before they would take his word. He looked the part too, in workmen's dungaree coveralls. He was not casing the houses, he explained to the sergeant, but was lingering on the sidewalks hoping somebody would walk out of a house and he could then beg for employment. Why didn't he knock at the door if he wanted to talk to the owners? Because he was scared. What if the owner opened the door, saw his Zulu face and thought this was an attack, and shot him point blank?

It was late in the evening when Em-Pee was released, and only after the precinct got too occupied with a gang of real criminals, bleeding everywhere after brawling over the spoils of a robbery.

He makes sure the rhythms of the law are no longer within earshot before he walks out of the park. He is tempted to stroll on Madison Avenue one more time before walking back home. Hopefully he will not be arrested today. He made a point of changing into decent clothing before departing his tenement with Davis – the top hat, buffed shoes and frock coat he used to wear when Aoife forced him to go to church. Surely even the dense New York Police Department officers will not mistake such a gentleman for a loiterer.

If only there was a way of finding out where the human curiosities that used to be at Madison Square Park have moved to.

'Hey! Papa!' The voice is unfamiliar. But there is no one else around, so he must be the 'father' who's being called. He turns slowly, and there she is. The Dinka Princess. She is standing on the sidewalk in front of the brownstone mansion. She is nothing like the purple Snow Princess he remembers. Or has dreamed about. She is barefoot and wears a calico dress that used to be white but has now become fawn. She is a bit unkempt, her hair uncombed. He walks towards her. Shaking.

'They didn't arrest you today?' she asks.

'You saw that?'

'From the window up there, yes. It was quite funny. We laughed about it.'

'You and who?'

'Me and Maria-Magdalena.'

'I was looking for you when I was arrested, and you find it funny?'

'I see you every day walking in front of my house. I think it's funny. I told Maria-Magdalena about you.'

This makes him angry. But she seems oblivious to it all. She stretches her hand towards him. She is holding a card. He hesitates.

'Come on. Take it, Papa. It's yours,' she says.

He takes it. And stares at it. His eyes widen when he realises it is a photograph of him. He is a silhouette because of the snow that surrounds him, and his facial features are not identifiable. But it is him all right. The outline of his head, the posture, the stance, it is him.

'Sorry it's so bad,' she says. 'It's the snow's fault. Also, I was still learning that time. I'm much better now. If you allow me, I can take you a much better picture.'

Em-Pee is amazed at this girl who spends her days in a cage as a human curiosity but is also a photographer. He has never met a real-life photographer before, and this is the first photograph of himself ever.

A middle-aged White woman in a voluminous blue dress, white apron and white bonnet appears at the door. 'Acol!' she calls in a rough voice.

'Maria-Magdalena?' asks Em-Pee.

She nods, yes.

'Acol!'

The Dinka Princess ignores her.

'Acol is your name?'

'Yes. But she is the only one who uses it. Others call me Dinkie. When she calls me Dinkie, I ignore her until she uses my real name, Acol.'

'But you are ignoring her now, and she's calling you Acol.'

Maria-Magdalena walks down the steps in a huff. She

grabs Acol by the arm and pulls her up the stairs, all the while admonishing her that she is a naughty girl who will put her in trouble again with Monsieur Duval if she keeps on playing in the street. Before they enter the house Em-Pee hears Maria-Magdalena ask Acol, 'Did he like the picture?' He can't hear what the answer is, but both women giggle as they enter the house and shut the heavy timber-and-iron door behind them.

Back at Five Points he spends the evening gazing at the photograph of himself silhouetted by snow. Only he knows it is snow. To anyone else it is just a dark human figure on a white background.

* * *

Maria-Magdalena has worked for Monsieur Duval and his Duval Ethnological Expositions for many years – from the time she was a blushing bride in her early twenties. Her late husband managed the company when it was still big, with many acts and varied exhibits, before it whittled down to the one display of Dinkie the Dinka Princess. The fall of the company due to Duval's love of bourbon and poker is a story for another day. After her husband's passing, Maria-Magdalena stayed with the company and doubled as Duval's housekeeper. Now her sole job is to look after Dinkie, or Acol, as she prefers to be called.

She shares her story; Em-Pee shares his too, as he enjoys buttered bread with tea and German sausages. His odyssey from kwaZulu to Cape Town, and then to London; the voyage to New York and the glorious performances with The Great Farini. He does not say anything about the loneliness and the struggles of diminishing Zulu stardom, though he does mention Aoife and Mavo in passing. She is fascinated by it all.

She is a good listener, but when it is her turn she does not hesitate to share bits of her life. Her people came from the Ottoman Empire, though her memory of her life there is vague. In any event, it is not what interests Em-Pee. He wants to know about the life today. About Acol.

Maria-Magdalena is grateful for the company, the relief from boredom while Acol is working and Monsieur Duval is out pursuing either business or pleasure prospects. Em-Pee came one day and knocked at the door. He was tired of skulking outside, hoping Acol would come out. The knowledge that she might be watching at the window and laughing at him emboldened him, so he walked up the steps and knocked. If the owner was there, well, he would deal with that then. The door was opened by Maria-Magdalena, who invited him in after pretending she was upset that he had the bravado to disturb her peace uninvited. She offered him a cup of chicken broth.

'Just for five minutes,' she said, 'and you must leave before Acol and the servants who supervise the exhibit or the master return and find you here.'

Five minutes became an hour.

He came again a few days later. And again. On one occasion Acol was there. But she did not talk to him. She merely nodded and went to her room. Maria-Magdalena explained to him that Acol was always in a bad mood when she came back from work, perhaps because her work entailed sitting in a cramped cage for hours on end while men ogled her. And masturbated to the fantasy of her, Em-Pee added in his mind, not voicing that thought.

Today he is determined to stay until Acol returns from work, and to talk to her.

'Maybe she will take you another photograph,' says Maria-Magdalena. 'You are the only person I know that she has photographed. She takes pictures only of insects and birds and trees and flowers and the like.'

'How does a girl living in her circumstances have the wherewithal to take photographs?' Em-Pee wonders aloud. She is using an old Scovill camera that she bought from her master, Maria-Magdalena tells him.

'At first she stole the camera after watching Monsieur Duval take pictures and process them in his darkroom. When he was particularly happy, maybe because the Dinka Princess exhibit brought in a lot of money that day, he taught her how to take pictures and how to develop them.'

Em-Pee goes home feeling buoyant, even though Acol did not spend much time talking to him. She kept on referring to him as papa or mister or sir, and seems to be emphasising that she sees him as no more than a father figure. Indeed, she could easily have been his daughter if he had married when men of his age were accumulating cattle wealth and taking wives instead of gallivanting around the world playing silly games for the pleasure of White people.

As soon as he walks into his tenement he reaches for the photograph and caresses it. Now that he knows the history of the photographer, especially that he is the only human being she has ever photographed, he feels this picture is much more precious than he had imagined.

Maybe he is more than just a father figure to her. Maybe it is a signal that she is attracted to him.

The next day Em-Pee makes a point of finishing early with Davis. Once more he dons his Sunday best and goes to Madison Avenue.

'Monsieur Duval has gone to Chicago for a few days,' says Maria-Magdalena. 'I've arranged that you take Acol with you for the night so that she can see how other Black folk live in Five Points.'

'Is that Acol's wish or yours?' asks Em-Pee, fearing that

he might be burdened with a woman who does not want to be with him.

'It is my idea,' says Acol, standing at the kitchen door. 'I am ready when you are.' Acol then turns to Maria-Magdalena and says sternly, 'No one must ever know about this or they will tell Monsieur Duval. That will be the end of you because you are supposed to keep me prisoner here.'

She is silent for the forty minutes it takes them to get to Mulberry Bend. He tries very hard to have some conversation, but all she does is grunt a yes or no without any elaboration.

She is the first woman he has had in his tenement since Aoife left. He does not know what to do with her. How do you entertain an uncommunicative girl? An ephemeral girl, who sometimes doesn't seem to be there at all? Does she want them to go out, perhaps, and have a drink and grub at a neighbourhood Irish pub? He makes the suggestion and she says no, she would rather stay in the room. She does not want the crowds; she sees enough of them to last her a lifetime when she is in the cage being ogled.

He leaves her for a while and comes back with some colcannon and beef stew from The Chop House. He gives her the food in a bowl, but she merely toys with it with a spoon without really eating it. After a while she declares she is not hungry and puts the bowl on the table.

She takes out a book and places it on the table. It is a tattered penny dreadful titled *Black Bess*.

'Wanna read?' asks Em-Pee.

'I can't read. My jailer reads it for me sometimes.'

'Jailer?'

'Maria-Magdalena.'

'I can read it for you.'

'Please.'

He moves closer to the smoky oil lamp and gingerly opens the pages, mindful that they do not fall out. He reads aloud about the outlaw Dick Turpin. Em-Pee is horrified that this character commits robberies and murder, breaking into farmhouses and stealing property, but Acol seems to be relishing it all. She even giggles when Turpin is chased by military men, mounts his horse Black Bess and gallops away, leaving everyone in the dust.

'You enjoy this sort of thing?' asks Em-Pee.

'Why not?'

'Isn't it for boys?'

'Who says?'

'Too savage for a young lady.'

'Isn't what they call us? Savages?'

He reads on. Right up to the end. She is already dozing off, but her face reflects nothing but bliss.

He leads her to the bed. She quickly gets under the blanket without taking off her clothes. He, on the other hand, strips naked and gets into bed beside her. He holds her in his arms. After a sporadic exchange of awkward compliments followed by moments of silence, he kisses her. She kisses him back. In no time she is all passion, kissing him so voraciously that his limbs quiver, not with anticipation but with fear. He stops. He does not know what the source of his fear is. But she takes the initiative and kisses him. It's not just a peck on the cheek or on the lips. She presses her open lips hard on his, breathing heavily. And he responds likewise.

They continue for a long time, until he cannot help it any more. She wants us to make love, he thinks. His hands frantically grope, searching for the drawstring of her drawers. He can't find it. She removes his hand, shaking her head, no. They kiss again, even more passionately than before. There is no way he can walk away from this; she may not be pleased with him. She does seem to want them to make love. He tries to reach for the drawstring again, to no avail. Then he gropes her crotch, hoping to find the overlap. She removes his hand firmly, with a hint of anger. But not before he concludes there is neither a drawstring nor an overlap. It obviously is not one of those old-fashioned split-legging drawers with an overlap that his wife wore.

As his hands caress her body he realises that she is wearing one of those combinations – a camisole bodice attached to drawers. How does she afford such classy undergarments? She's a captive girl who lives in a cage for most of the day. Everything she wears would be a hand-me-down from the ladies of the house. Poor women like her go without this new-fangled habit of wearing undergarments. But he has no time to dwell on these questions or to seek an answer. He wants her.

'Please take it off,' he pleads.

'No, I feel safe with it on,' she whispers.

All he can do is rest his stiff member on her crotch. She responds by moving her hips in a frenetic lovemaking motion. He humps gently, and they make frottage love while she remains clothed. She seems to enjoy it and moans as though this is penetrative sex. He tells her he is about to come, and she says, 'Please don't. I'll be wearing these drawers again tomorrow.' He respects her wishes and climbs down from her. He is still erect though. He feels her hand looking for his manhood. Of her own volition she grabs it, stiff and throbbing as if it has a heart of its own, and masturbates it vigorously until he ejaculates.

'Thank you, thank you,' he says as she cleans the semen off her hand on his belly. 'It is just as good as penetration. You made me very happy.'

She quickly turns her back on him and says, 'No, it is not just as good. You're just saying that.'

He holds her and rocks her like a baby. I've violated her, the words ring in his head. I've violated her. She could have been my daughter. I have violated her.

In the morning she declines breakfast. As he walks her home, he tells her he loves her and is determined to liberate her from Duval.

'What hold does he have on you?' he asks.

'He owns me,' she says.

'No one owns anyone any more. You don't have to go back to Duval. What can he do about it? Come on, stay with me.'

She does not respond. And for the rest of the way they walk in silence. About two blocks from Monsieur Duval's mansion she urges him to return.

She would rather walk alone. She doesn't want to be seen with him.

For many days after this encounter he is tortured by it. A deep sense of shame prevents him from going anywhere near the brownstone mansions. He is not sure what to make of his relationship with her. Are they lovers?

Or is he a dirty old man who took advantage of a trusting girl in search of a father figure? And what was that lovemaking about? He wonders why she limited it to the intercrural. Could she be one of those young women who are preserving their maidenhood for marriage? If that was the case he would be even more ashamed of himself. Perhaps he misread the signs. Perhaps she does not love him. But she did kiss him back, didn't she? They kissed passionately. In some ways she was proactive, otherwise he would not have gone on. He is attacked by guilt. Did he use this girl? Did he force himself on her? Did he rape her?

He feels dirty.

7

New York City — November 1887
Courtship

Skildore Skolnik sits in front of a roaring fire, rocking his chair gently as he reads the play script. Davis and Em-Pee stare at him expectantly, occasionally glancing at each other with question marks in their eyes whenever the producer frowns. The more he reads, the more he frowns, and the more Davis's face contorts with worry.

'Obviously you're no writers,' says Skolnik finally.

'I did my best, given the circumstances,' says Davis.

'It's a bloody mess. The story is all over the place.'

'But that's how it happened,' says Em-Pee. 'All over.'

'I don't give a flying tart how it happened. I want a story. There is no story here. This has potential though. This can be a great musical play if you take my advice.'

At this Davis smiles and Em-Pee scowls.

Skolnik looks at him suspiciously. 'You don't think what I am saying makes sense?' he asks, glaring at Em-Pee.

'Yes, sir, I don't think it makes sense,' says Em-Pee innocently.

Davis elbows him in the back so hard he staggers. He realises he might have said the wrong thing.

'What I'm trying to say, sir, is that there is a story there. It is the story of my people. I know it first-hand because I was there for most of it.'

Skolnik says there are quite a few things he likes in the play. But the savages cannot be left with ultimate victory. Yes, in Isandlwana they won, but the play must extend to Ulundi and depict the defeat of the savage king. Only then will the audiences walk out of Niblo's satisfied.

'The Great Farini said King Cetshwayo became popular with White people because he defeated a superior civilisation,' says Em-Pee. 'Why can't we let Isandlwana be Isandlwana in all its glory?'

'With due respect to your Farini, he knows nothing about theatre,' says Skolnik, turning down the corners of his mouth contemptuously. 'This is theatre. This is no freak show.'

Skolnik says a lot of fictionalisation must be added. The savage king must be possessed by demons – his conscience devouring him to a point of madness – for biting the benevolent British hand that fed him. It is at this point of madness that British soldiers come and kill him at his royal palace in Ulundi.

Em-Pee protests once more. 'But that's not how Cetshwayo died.'

'If you want authenticity you are in the wrong business,' Davis pipes up.

'I don't give a flying tart for authenticity,' says Skolnik. 'I want a working story, a Shakespearean tragedy. You take it or leave it.'

He indicates that the meeting is over. As they walk out he says to Davis, 'Next time don't come with the Zulu. He argues too much.'

As soon as they get outside, Davis says, 'Skildore Skolnik is not Slaw. You don't just talk to him anyhow you like. He doesn't like uppity Negroes.'

He then turns his back on him and limps away.

Em-Pee stands there for a while looking at him, puzzled.

Then he yells after him. 'I'm not an uppity Negro! I'm an *uppity* Zulu.' He stresses *uppity*, enunciating each syllable.

*   *   *

Maria-Magdalena has arranged that Acol and Em-Pee meet at the nearby park – where he first saw her as a caged princess. Maria-Magdalena has done it twice since that night, five months ago, when she let Em-Pee take Acol to Five Points so that she could learn how Black people lived.

After Em-Pee had squirmed in shame for a few days,

he couldn't help but return to Monsieur Duval's mansion.

At first, he stopped on the sidewalk and gazed at the windows upstairs, one of which he hoped would be Acol's or Maria-Magdalena's bedroom. He lingered for an hour or so and then left. The next day he came with a determination to knock at the door. But he froze for a while just when his knuckles were about to hit the wooden panel, and then left. On the third attempt he froze again, but Maria-Magdalena swung the door open and glared at him.

'What did you do to the girl?' she asked, not even waiting for him to complete a timid greeting.

'Nothing. I love her,' said Em-Pee.

'You cannot love her, you will not love her, she is not meant to be loved.'

Em-Pee was dumbfounded.

'I sent her with you because I thought you were a responsible adult family man,' she added.

'I am an adult family man. What did she say I did to her?'

'I don't know. She does not want to talk about it. But she says it was just the two of you. The whole night? No wife? No child? You told me you're married and have a child. You lied to me.'

'I do have a child, yes, but I no longer have a wife. She ran away with the circus.'

Maria-Magdalena could not help but laugh. 'People do that in real life?'

Em-Pee looked pained. He did not understand what was funny about being deserted for a circus.

Maria-Magdalena suddenly became serious again and glared into his eyes. 'What makes you think you can love Acol and live?'

He stood there as if mesmerised by her question. She invited him in for a cup of bean-and-bone soup. She put some gin in hers, claiming that it was medicine for her weak knees. Em-Pee was no fool; he knew the smell of gin and said so.

'Of course, it is gin,' she said. 'But it is knee medicine too.'

Em-Pee said he wanted to try some for his knees too, in case they gave him problems in future. He'd never thought anyone would want to mess up such a delicacy as bean-and-bone soup with alcohol. Not being a regular imbiber, soon his knees were becoming jelly instead of stronger. And soon the two were full of nothing but laughter and silliness.

It was during this warm imbibing session that the plan was hatched: when the situation allowed, Maria-Magdalena would take Acol to Madison Square Park where they could meet – provided Acol wanted to see him.

This brought so much joy to Em-Pee that even Slaw

and Samson noticed the change. When they danced at a Tenderloin outdoor venue, with Mavo as the drummer boy, he recaptured the flair he used to have in kwaZulu, before his soul had been battered by the vulgar dances of London and the failures of New York. He was graceful in his gyrations, in his high-kicking jinks, in his foot-stomping. They did not know it was for Acol he was dancing.

He had summoned her to stand in the front row, and she was clapping her hands excitedly. Seen only by him, she gave him more power, more inspiration, more agility, more stamina. She was the muse he discovered he could invoke on demand, and there the muse was, swaying in front of him, with thick, pursed red lips and wide smiling eyes with the whitest of sclera and the blackest of irises. Her tall limbs yearned for a dance, but she dared not steal his thunder. Remember, this was his narrative; his to control. Hers was only to inspire him to greater heights. She only swayed gently, her knobbly knees almost knocking against each other.

Soon he was in full flight, dancing on top of the buildings, spinning on one building and then, with the longest of strides ever seen in a human being, jumping to the next and waving his shield high up to the heavens and down to the roof in the rhythmic manner of isizingili dance, and then throwing himself down and spinning on his stomach, and then diving to another building and stomping his feet in the manner of isishameni dance.

He looked down and saw his dance partners, Slaw and Samson, continuing with the rhythms of the different dances, trying hard to keep up with him, drenched in sweat despite the chill of the November air. He saw the drummer boy beating the drumhead like a demented spirit. Acol hovered silently above, egging him on. It was for Acol that he was dancing, despite the presence of the spectators, whose numbers had grown to almost a hundred. They were all agog with exhilaration and wonderment.

Samson blew a long whistle and Mavo stopped the drumming with a final heavenly thud. The dance cannot go on forever. Em-Pee dropped to the ground, and the other dancers did likewise. The spectators burst into wild cheers and applause.

'Em-Pee, you have saved the Friendly Zulus,' said Slaw, breathlessly.

'What possessed you?' asked Samson, out of breath as well.

'Acol,' said Em-Pee, breathing as easily as one who had not danced a single step that day.

No one knew what he was talking about.

* * *

At the park Maria-Magdalena hovers as Em-Pee and Acol sit on a bench. She is always within earshot, to Em-Pee's consternation, and has told them she must be around because a park warden may kick them out, thinking they are vagrants. Acol tells Em-Pee that the only reason Maria-Magdalena is here is because she is her jailer. She is always trailing her, even when she comes here on her own to take pictures of the flowers.

'Did I rape you?' asks Em-Pee abruptly. It is almost a whisper and he is shaking, dreading the answer.

'When?' She is not whispering back. She is so loud that Em-Pee takes a quick look at Maria-Magdalena. But the jailer is pretending to read a penny dreadful while standing only a few feet away. Em-Pee wonders for how long she will be on her feet. Obviously, her gin works wonders for her knees. He wishes she would find a bench some yards away and truly enjoy her penny dreadful.

'When? What do you mean, when? When could it have been possible?'

She shakes her head, no, and says, 'I helped you along.'

Em-Pee is greatly relieved. But soon he goes back to wondering why she didn't allow them to totally consummate the relationship that night. The doubts return. Maybe she does not see him as a lover at all. Perhaps she thinks he's too old to allow him to penetrate her. That must be it. He is too old. The shame returns with the doubts. He imagines her father, wherever he might be, probably in his forties too, looking at him as a dirty old man who uses little girls. Or maybe it really has nothing to do with him at all. Maybe she has physical problems. Maybe moral issues. Maybe she's just a teenager who has never known a man biblically before. But what her hands did to him that night spoke of experience. Maybe.

How he wishes she would express her feelings in words, what she thinks, what she wants and doesn't want, and why. Most of all, how she feels about him. He has told her so many times that he loves her. And all she says is 'thank you'. Or, when pressed further, she says 'it's mutual'.

'I dance for you,' announces Em-Pee, gazing at her as if he is expecting praise or at least gratitude.

'Please don't,' she says, horrified.

'Oh no, I don't mean now. I mean, at my performances with the Friendly Zulus. I perform the dances of my people for you.'

'But I am not there to see them.'

'Yep. But I dance for you still. I conjure you up and you are there, and I dance for you.'

She looks at him curiously, and then says, 'I sit in my cage for you too.'

'You're bullshitting.'

'I am not. If you can dance for me at your work when I am not there, I can sit for you when you are not there at my work too. Tit for tat.'

'As if it hurts.'

'It hurts too. I don't want to be idealised.'

'But I do. You are my muse. You know what that is?'

'I don't want to be a muse. It's too heavy a burden to carry.'

'Okay, I just want to marry you then. You don't have to be a muse or anything. Just marry me.'

This unsettles Maria-Magdalena and she moves closer, pretending to admire a winter bloom on a nearby leather-leaf mahonia shrub. She forces out a concocted cough to warn them she is here, can hear everything and does not approve of the direction of the conversation. Acol, on the other hand, is expressionless, as if nothing earth-shattering has been said.

'Don't you think it's a good idea?'

She looks at Maria-Magdalena and shakes her head, no. He feels frustrated that he has no way of knowing how she feels. Sometimes it is just yes, or no, and nothing beyond that. She communicates in one-word answers, or no answers at all, making it difficult for him to fathom her. He idealises her, and he now realises she has been resenting that in her uncommunicative way, until she blurted it out today. Perhaps she should have added that all she wants in the world is to be left alone to spend her days in the crowded solitude of her cage. Her actions and non-actions seem to be saying that. The fact that she is so cold and distant from his idolisation.

But he has raised the topic. There is no turning back.

'I find it difficult to believe a nubile Nubian Princess like you has no suitors and does not want to entertain even one.'

'I vowed never to marry,' she says curtly.

They are silent for a while. Maria-Magdalena hovers even closer, indicating that it is time to go. But the man and the woman sit there defiantly, neither making the slightest attempt to stand up.

'You have no business idealising me,' she blurts out. 'You scare me when you idealise me. You make me afraid of you. It is creepy to be idealised like this. I am not the person you have created in your imagination.'

This is the longest sentiment he has heard her express, and it leaves him dumbfounded. But also hopeful that it augurs more coherent communication in their future.

'You heard her,' says Maria-Magdalena.

'How can there be any meaningful courtship in your presence?'

'She has no time for courtship.'

'But I love her. Not for here. She does not belong in the world of the White man, which is a prison; all of it, not just her cage, all of it is a prison. I want to take her to my kingdom, to enjoy the Festival of the First Fruits with the free maidens of my land. I want to dance for her. Dance until she knows I am the one. Dance until I drop dead if she won't have me.'

Acol's eyes widen and she smiles the broadest smile he has ever seen on her, her teeth glistening in the winter sun. This encourages him, and he goes into a flight of fancy about the two First Fruits Festivals, which are highlights of the year. He and the other military men wear full battledress. Just before the summer solstice, which is about this time of the year but a different season from what they have in New York, is the time of ulwezi, when young men scour the coastal areas of the country for fresh new calabashes to be used for drinking potent beer from the season's first fruit of sorghum. They also bring back to the Royal Place the fibrous imizi plant from which the king's garment will be woven. It is also the time the warriors move to every corner of the kingdom collecting the soul of the nation in the form of natural substances that have been touched by or brushed against friends and foes, chiefs and generals, lovers and haters of the king and his kingdom. These materials, in the form of grass, wood, dirt or stone, are brought back to the hut at the centre of isigodlo, and are used to rejuvenate the iNkatha, the conceptual-art piece of natural and found objects where the king sits when he wants to listen to himself or is having his ceremonial ablutions. During all this time, young men and young women separately practise songs for the feasting to come.

All these activities culminate in the big festival, the uzibandlela, which is the core of the First Fruits rituals.

Acol, with her long limbs and the kind of height that has never been seen on any woman or perhaps man of the amaZulu people, leads the dances of her regiment. The song is meant to entice the king: 'Woza, Nkosi, woza lapha!' 'Come hither, King, come over here!' Em-Pee – actually, he is no longer Em-Pee now but Mpiyezintombi, He-Who-Washed-His-Spear-With-The-Blood-Of-A-Lion – smiles to himself as he stands in the company of warriors waiting for their turn to dance. He knows that Acol is his, and the king has no chance at all. Even John Dunn would have no chance at all with Acol if he were still there. Not after all the experiences Acol has had in being caged by White men.

The turn for the warriors to dance arrives. They also dance according to their regiments, each trying to outdo the previous one in its prowess. They all want to impress the king. But Mpiyezintombi, leading his regiment, wants to impress only Acol. He dances facing in her direction, much to the annoyance of the grandees, who have been looking at her with desire hanging from their mouths, actually salivating. He breaks away from the rest of the dancing warriors, and dances in front of Acol.

Maria-Magdalena is scandalised. Acol stands up from the bench and backs away from his gyrating movements. He suddenly stops, ashamed of himself. He is not at Ondini, the capital of kwaZulu, but in Madison Square Park.

'It is different from the ways of my Dinka people, but

somehow it relates, as if it is a world not far removed from them,' says Acol.

At least his flight of fancy to the world of his fathers has drawn her out of her shell. Even her face has lost its tension. It is smooth but not taut.

'Tell me about it, what you remember of it, your own First Fruits Festival,' he says to Acol.

Even Maria-Magdalena seems keen to know. She sits on the bench as if she has been invited into their company and pays attention. Em-Pee wonders why she never attempted to find out about Acol's pre-captivity life, if she was interested at all.

'I don't remember anything like that.'

But she remembers huts built on stilts. The land that is flatter than any flatness that you have ever seen in this country, the flatness that you can follow right up to the entrance to thick forests. Lush green lands for miles on end until you get to the whiteness of the desert sand. She remembers the land more than anything. The land. And the landscape. Honey and butterflies.

Acol adds, 'Sometimes I come here to take photos of squirrels and rockeries and flowers in spring. And then I remember myself as a little girl, and I will the bees and the butterflies to hover above my head. I walk out of the park with the bees and butterflies following me.'

'You never told me that,' says Maria-Magdalena, obviously feeling jealous that she has not been part of this story for all these years and he is. 'I've never seen no bees!'

'Well, I have,' says Acol adamantly.

She talks! Now she talks!

And fishing parties. She remembers fishing parties. She is disappointed when Em-Pee tells her there are no fishing parties in kwaZulu; amaZulu do not eat fish. How would she dance in valleys where rivers and seas don't overflow with fish? She learns they are teeming with fish all right, but fish are not part of what amaZulu consider a delicacy. This is disappointing. But it is their problem, not hers.

Her father was the Master of the Fishing Spear. He was endowed by Divinity to look after the fish in the river that passed through his village. She remembers women of her village, young and old, spending days on end at the river, catching and drying fish, all to song and dance.

Sometimes the women fought among themselves, particularly older women sickened by the disrespect of the younger ones. And the river deities became angry. The Master of the Fishing Spear was angry because the deities of the river were angry. He waved his fishing spear, uttering incantations, and all the fish swam upstream to other rivers where they were not disrespected. When that happened, the village women came to Alcol's home bearing gifts of fish to sue for peace. They also presented the Master of the Fishing Spear with one dance after another, until he relented and waved the spear with more incantations. Soon the fish flowed back to the river.

Those were the most wonderful moments of her young life, because the sound of songs and drums and dance reverberated through the valleys, and the aroma of fish cooked in a variety of ways permeated the village.

Soon Em-Pee's eyes are misty with tears of nostalgia for a world he has never known. She is taken aback, thinking she has said something wrong. Maria-Magdalena decides to take discipline into her hands, and says sternly, 'I do not think Monsieur Duval will be happy to hear that your head is full of all these heathen things. You must wash your tongue with soap and water as soon as you get into the house.'

At this, she lifts Acol up with both hands, forcing her to stand. But Em-Pee will not let her go and he stands in front of them.

'I love her,' he says to Maria-Magdalena. Turning to Acol he repeats, 'I love you.'

'Get out of our way!' screeches Maria-Magdalena.

'You must say something, Acol. I love you. You can't be silent.'

'It is mutual,' says Acol softly.

Both women look amazed when this enrages Em-Pee. They are oblivious of his frustration at being unable to draw the words 'I love you too' from her.

'It is mutual? What does that even mean? I say *I* love you; you tell me it is mutual?'

'What do you want from me?'

'I love you.'

'And now you are throwing a tantrum about it? What kind of a man is this?' says Maria-Magdalena.

'Love you too,' Acol says with great difficulty.

He's still not satisfied. She has not taken ownership of her feelings. It is all so impersonal with the absence of 'I'. But she is adamant she won't go a single step beyond that. It is her turn now to jerk her jailer by the sleeve, urging them to go.

'You will never get the "I" from her,' says Maria-Magdalena, wagging her finger as they walk away. 'It would be the death of you if you did.'

Em-Pee can only fold his arms and take a deep breath as he watches them go.

She is becoming more and more beautiful as she is moving further away from him.

8

New York City – July/August 1889
The Aesthetic of Dignity

This is why he stayed away for almost seventeen months. In the long run you cannot love what does not return your love, whether we are talking of sentient or sapient beings, animate or inanimate objects. Reciprocity comes in many ways, some of which are silent. At some point unrequited love turns to hate, for the two passions are closely related. Sometimes the line that divides them is so blurry it is difficult to see.

She has receded as a woman but has remained as a muse. The three-man dance of the Friendly Zulus continues at the Tenderloin, at both outdoor and indoor venues. Em-Pee summons Acol and dances for her. He goes into flight and mesmerises the spectators with a variety of time-honoured dances of amaZulu people in all their authenticity, delving into variations of umzansi and khwexa once popularised by warriors and maidens of uKhahlamba Mountains, isizingili and isishameni, much beloved in uMsinga, and changing to other movements such as isicathamiya, yet to be invented by the progeny in decades and centuries to come. That is the power of her musing; it draws the future from his sinews.

She fuels his flight, yet he hates her. Even as she materialises at every angle he turns, clapping her hands and egging him on, he hates her with a passion.

His dance partners would hate him too if his agility had not changed their fortunes. He is showing off and exposing their inferior skill. But they can live with that. As long as this gives them more engagements in the nightclubs, saloons and dance halls of the Tenderloin. Even though in many instances they are employed as a supporting act to acts that are more vaudeville, or in smaller clubs and bordellos that are more risqué, the three men have recovered their livelihood. Even Samson is no longer heard voicing his regret for having left The Great Farini and works fewer shifts as a bordello security guard.

Em-Pee has told them to whom the success should be attributed. A caged woman who was known as Dinkie the Dinka Princess before he got to know her as Acol, so named by her father after his favourite black cow. In the taverns over beer after the performances he tells them of his encounters with this woman, and how he has absolutely failed to fathom her. But he does not tell them of the one encounter, the impenetrable night. He will not be laughed at by these crude jokers for not being savvy enough to have his way with a woman delivered by the gods to his bed for the night. He tells them about her influence as a muse, and how he now hates her, though he will continue to exploit her as the proverbial feminine part of himself.

Sometimes Davis joins them for a drink. They ask him about The Wild Zulu. His act is still going strong after six years, he tells them, though he seems reluctant to say much about it. They long moved from Longacre Square to an indoor venue, but he doesn't want to say where. Em-Pee suspects things are not as rosy as Davis pretends. Otherwise why has he become so close to Slaw, who really has nothing to offer, and why is he showing more enthusiasm for the Cetshwayo Project, as they now call it? Why is he showing so much interest in The Friendly Zulus, as if he wants a piece of the action?

Despite the tension between them, Em-Pee and Davis meet intermittently, sometimes at Five Points, and at others at a convenient tavern, but never at Davis's mansion. Davis is no longer limping. Instead he has a broken arm in a sling, which makes writing a bit difficult. He says he slipped and rolled down a spiral staircase. He must be extremely accident prone.

This morning at Em-Pee's tenement, Davis paces the tiny floor while Em-Pee sits on a rickety chair reading the script.

'What is this?' asks Em-Pee. 'I see monsters and little devils and demons that drive the savage king and imbue

148

him with evil powers? That's not my king. That's not the Cetshwayo I knew.'

'What part of *play* don't you understand?' asks Davis. 'It's a play. We are bloody playing.'

'Bloody? You've been keeping too much company with Slaw.'

'A great play must have morality lessons on good versus evil. Otherwise what's the point? The king and his generals represent evil, and the British and their commanders are a force for good.'

'Not where I come from,' says Em-Pee, getting agitated. 'We were a force for good, fighting to protect our lands and cattle against invaders.'

Davis tries very hard to mollify him. 'You and I know that,' he says gently. 'But Broadway audiences do not. They will not accept a situation where White Christian folks are accused of being evil, and heathens are the good guys.'

Em-Pee is still not satisfied. He grumbles under his breath. If the practice of theatre thrives on truth-twisting, then it is not for him.

'This is our big break, man,' says Davis, pleadingly now. 'I mean, your big opportunity. Your chance to be a hotshot Broadway actor in a play you assisted in writing. You heard Skildore will take nothing less. We need a motivating force for this king; without the devils and the demons we don't have that.'

'I am not going to have that in *my* play,' says Em-Pee with finality. He walks to the door, opens it and gestures to Davis that it's time to go.

'Your play? This is my play. I am the writer. You are merely the assistant.'

Em-Pee indicates that he has nothing more to add.

'I was going to make you rich, you know, just as I have made many other Zulus rich. Tell you what, I was talking with Slaw and Samson the other day. They told me about your Dinka person. I told Slaw I can put money down and we can buy her. We can make a lot of money.'

He does not seem to notice that Em-Pee is almost exploding with rage.

'I know her owner. Duval. He's my neighbour. A good-for-nothing bourbon-soaked gambler. We can negotiate a good price for your Dinka person, including the wagon, the mule and the cage. She can sit in the cage during the day making money for us, and you can have her all to yourself at night.'

He is wide-eyed when Em-Pee pounces on him, grabs him by the scruff of the neck, and pushes him out. After shutting the door behind him, Em-Pee stands there for a while, hyperventilating, uttering in his language invective whose translation you wouldn't want to know.

* * *

It didn't take long for the muse to recede after the woman had receded. For days she had become fainter, until she refused to be summoned. Em-Pee's foot-stomping became weaker and unsteadier with each performance. This coincided with the return of The Great Farini to Madison Square Garden, the glorious venue on the north-east corner of East 26th Street and Madison Avenue, rather than Madison Square Park itself, where Dinkie the Dinka Princess used to be displayed before the park was re-vamped.

Fans deserted Em-Pee's troupe for Farini's Zulus, who performed blood-curdling savage dances, rather than the namby-pamby Friendly Zulus who did not have a single ferocious bone in their bodies, and whose dances had become tired and limp.

To add to their woes, Samson deserted them. He returned to the fold of The Great Farini, and the funambulist welcomed him back, if only to spite the biggest traitors of all time, Slaw and Em-Pee.

The Friendly Zulus had no choice but to limp on as a two-man troupe. They could not come up with any gimmick that they could sell, and Slaw missed the creative genius of Davis, the only man he thought could save them. After all, he was the impresario who conceived The Wild Zulu. But Davis had extricated himself from their company and had not been seen for almost a month.

Today is not much different. Supplies are running

short and The Friendly Zulus must busk. Em-Pee tries to get Mavo from the Industrial House to drum for them, but he claims his hands are sore from working on one or other machine. He has been making quite a few excuses lately. Sometimes a headache or a stomach ache or a dizzy spell, even though Em-Pee had just seen him jump about playing catch with the other boys before he spotted his father.

Em-Pee busks with Slaw. Just the two of them. Perhaps they should change their name to The Black and White Zulus. That might be a new selling point. He will try to sell the idea to Slaw. Slaw. He wonders what keeps him loyal to a failing outfit. Perhaps it's not loyalty. Lack of choice? He is sure he would return to The Great Farini in a jiffy if the maestro would have him. Perhaps he was hoping to get closer to Davis, get a piece of his action, and become a mogul with a brownstone mansion on Madison Avenue.

'You dance like a White Zulu lately, guv,' says Slaw, self-satisfied that for a change he is the better dancer.

'Shut up; let's dance,' says Em-Pee, and starts singing a war chant, clapping his hands for rhythm.

Slaw responds to the chant and starts creeping around Em-Pee like a wild cat ready to pounce on its prey. Em-Pee stamps his feet hard on the sidewalk for more rhythm. Two or three spectators look on curiously. One gets bored and leaves after deciding nothing more exciting is likely to develop here. Three ragamuffins, perhaps Street Arabs, join the dance mockingly, and laugh as the dancers try to shoo them away.

A hansom cab stops on the pavement next to their sidewalk. The driver, still perched on his high seat, waves a letter at the dancers. Slaw jumps for it, and after a quick glance he hands it to Em-Pee. He scowls as he reads it. It is from Maria-Magdalena. He must come quickly. Acol wants to see him. He had vowed to forget about Acol. But he must go. Acol is calling. He jumps into the cab without further ado. Slaw reaches for the hat containing two measly coins on the sidewalk, and holds on to the cab, trying to climb on too.

'My instructions are that I am picking up one gentle-man, not two, sir,' says the driver. 'The Black one.'

Slaw ignores him and sits next to Em-Pee. The driver shakes his head and flicks the horse into a canter.

'What's this all about, guv?'

Em-Pee does not respond. They are silent for the rest of the way.

Maria-Magdalena is waiting outside the mansion. 'She's at the park,' she says and dismisses the cab driver.

It is Em-Pee's turn to ask what this is all about. Instead of explaining, Maria-Magdalena turns to Slaw, who is tagging along, and asks, 'Who's this one?'

'I'm Czeslaw Trzetrzelewska, at your service, ma'am,' says Slaw, giving a polite bow.

'He talks funny,' says Maria-Magdalena.

"'Cause am a Londoner, ma'am, born and bred.'

At the park Acol is aiming her ancient Scovill at a bug perched on a leaf.

'There she is, wasting pictures on leaves and bugs when there are people to photograph,' says Maria-Magdalena.

Acol shushes them; they will frighten her subject. This nonchalant reception is not what Em-Pee expected. She summoned him. He is here despite himself. He stands to attention. And all her focus is on a bug?

When Acol is done taking a picture to her satisfaction, she signals Em-Pee to follow her and they move to a bench further away. Slaw is about to follow them but Maria-Magdalena stops him and they find another place to sit.

'Last time, you forced me to remember,' says Acol as soon as they are sitting on the bench.

'I didn't think the journey we took to your land of butterflies and honey was forced on you,' says Em-Pee. 'You seemed to flow into it.'

'My body rebels against remembering. Except for the butterflies and honey, which I couldn't connect to anything, I have never remembered until you remembered *your* First Fruits Festivals. Only then did my body relent and I could remember. I learned from you how to remember, without knowing I was learning. I realised after you were gone that I was a bad pupil and had forgotten as soon as you left. I want you to help me remember again. I long to remember.'

She says this with so much emotion that Em-Pee stares at her face closely, only to see lurking in her eyes, a film of unshed tears. They look like they will congeal and become glass if she does not allow them to roll down her cheeks.

He is disappointed, and his face cannot hide it. She is too involved in the anguish of her lack of memory to detect the disappointment. He had hoped she summoned him because she wanted him for himself. It does not do his ego much good to learn that she merely wanted him for his ability to make her conjure up her domaine perdu.

'How are they?' She opens her mouth and shows him her teeth. They are sparkling white, almost translucent at the edges. 'I had bread and tea for breakfast. Tea and coffee stain my teeth. I hate to stain my teeth.'

'I don't see any staining at all. Your teeth are the most beautiful I have ever seen on any person.'

Maria-Magdalena may keep the distance but will never lose the line of sight. Her attention is divided in three directions – her charge Acol, a penny dreadful, and Slaw who, Em-Pee suspects, is irritating her like he always does him with his boastful prattle. She must be trying to figure out what Acol is doing showing her teeth to the man. Some kind of African flirting, perhaps?

'I hate them,' says Acol. 'Not all of them. The bottom ones. The six bottom front ones.'

They should have been extracted when she was ten; now she remembers that's why she hates her teeth. Her body agrees to remember, with all the shaking and facial contortions that come with remembering. It would have been a great ceremony, having her teeth removed to join the ranks of the beautiful young ladies of her clan, whose major attribute of beauty was the lack of bottom front teeth.

The tooth-extraction ritual is performed with a fishing spear, and she, the daughter of the Master of the Fishing Spear, is ten and ready. And everything is ready. The doors of womanhood are about to open. But it is not to be. The Arab slavers come with guns and caravans of camels and abduct random members of families. They know the right time to invade, when the warriors of the village are out hunting or minding their cattle, and the women are tending to their groundnut, bean and sorghum fields. Only the young, the old and infirm, and the Master of the Fishing Spear are home. It is tooth-extraction day, so the family is home. Some members of the family are able to escape into the forests, but Acol, her father, her mother and an aunt are captured.

'It was all my father's fault,' says Acol. 'My aunt kept saying so throughout that journey to the north. A Jieng woman can nag as well as any and my aunt had flaming blades in her tongue.'

'A Jieng woman? She belonged to a different clan?' asks Em-Pee.

'The Jieng are my people. That is what we call ourselves. Or the Muonjang. We don't know the Dinka name. It came from outsiders, maybe the Arabs. We first heard we were Dinka when we were taken into captivity.'

The Arabs sell the family unit to a French entrepreneur, Monsieur Duval, and it becomes a star attraction at his Duval Ethnological Expositions in Paris.

'People come and stare at us. We have never known anything like this before. They just come and stare. And we just sit there and do nothing. Sometimes my mother plays with my hair, sometimes my father murmurs a story of some warrior conquest. Sometimes I doze off, and dream of playing in the river with my friends. My parents are both beautiful without the bottom front teeth.

I am the only ugly one with a mouth full of teeth. I close my mouth all the time. The crowds of Paris must not see that I am a Jieng girl with all her teeth intact.'

The aunt is sold to another company when her nagging is no longer entertaining. It seems to agitate the male exhibit. And that gets to the female and child exhibits as well. A sanguine exhibit works better than an agitated one. Parisian tourists, school children and even wedding parties must see only a serene family unit, self-satisfied to be sitting amid this glittering civilisation, away from the savagery of the jungle, being fed on a regular basis and getting fat as a result, without any cares in the world, just sitting there, long limbs curled on a Persian carpet. Apparently, this is not an ideal situation for the aunt. She keeps on nagging until they remove her.

The Master of the Fishing Spear takes the nagging with fortitude though. He knows it is, as she says, his fault they are in captivity. He converted to the God of the White man and became a Christian. He went from house to house calling himself Evangelist and urging the Jieng people to follow a certain Jesus Christ from a faraway city called Nazareth. The outrage at the behaviour of the Master of the Fishing Spear began on earth, with the scandalised elders. When the elders are outraged, the clan spirits, the yieth, are outraged too, because the man who has deserted Nhialic for a White God is the Master of the Fishing Spear himself. Even Deng, the closest Divinity to Nhialic, was outraged. He spoke in the voice of thunder to express his anger and struck the man's favourite bull with lightning. That was when everybody knew that the anger had gone far higher than just the yieth. It would even have gone to the highest plane, to Nhialic himself, if he had time to waste on the silly affairs of petty men.

Even after the bull was struck dead and its meat

could not be eaten, Evangelist evangelised, and people warned him that more calamity would befall the village. The fish warned him too, by migrating from the rivers to the swamps, where they committed suicide by drowning in the mud in their thousands. And the slavers came. And all was finished for the family of the Master of the Fishing Spear.

Even without the nagging aunt, the patriarch does not find peace within himself. He longs for death. Often, he speaks to himself as if he is back in the village. He moans and complains of the disrespect of the youth, as if he has suddenly transitioned into dotage. He curses his age-mates for leaving him alone with insolent children who now regard him as an imbecile because he is old and always complaining. He has taken the aunt's place and is nagging himself to a slow death.

Monsieur Duval extends his Duval Ethnological Expositions to New York City and exports the girl, leaving her parents behind, promising them that she would be back, or they would join her in America, depending on which works best. He invents the hugely successful Dinkie the Dinka Princess concept and she never sees her parents again. She hears they didn't survive long. She believes they died because she loved them. She shouldn't have loved them that much. Perhaps not at all.

'Hugely successful? I don't think so,' says Em-Pee.

'When you saw it at this park it was nothing. It is

on its last legs even now. I used to be a star attraction to thousands of spectators at Madison Square Garden.'

'You must be glad it's coming to an end,' says Em-Pee.

'It makes no difference,' she says.

It makes a difference to him. Perhaps soon it will be the end of her bondage. She won't be followed by a jailer everywhere she goes. The jailer. The last time he looked in her direction she was buried in her penny dreadful while Slaw sat next to her, arms folded, looking bored. But now he is dancing for her. He is clapping his hands, singing a pseudo-Zulu song and performing a silly jig in front of her bench. She is beside herself with laughter. Slaw is killing Maria-Magdalena with laughter.

Acol sees none of this. Her body is immersed in remembering. And in plotting her vengeance. The plotting starts in steerage during the voyage. She explores the depth of her soul and decides that people suffer not because of their sins but because of the sins of those close to them. It is all because, as the Jieng say, Nhialic has no tears. Nhialic is heartless. From now on she will depend solely on the power of her personal spirit, her jok. She will not appeal to the God of the White man, because he has no power over her as a Jieng woman. In the same way that she could not appeal to the God of the Arabs for salvation when they marched with the caravan of slavers. Each God has power only over his or her own people. Each God is a creation of his or her own people and can control only his or her own creators. Each God lives and dies inside his or her creator. Acol can only depend on her jok, because her jok is always with her.

'Why is Nhialic so disconnected from his people that she now has to depend on her own jok to avenge her shame?' Em-Pee wonders aloud, not particularly wanting to ask her because he does not think she will have an answer to that.

But she knows the answer. Every Jieng child knows the answer. It begins with creation. It happened in a distant epoch when Heaven and Earth were still in one place, in the same neighbourhood, separated only by a short rope. Nhialic was bored so he created the first woman ever, Abuk, and the first man, Garang. As Supreme Gods are wont to be, Nhialic was very stingy and allowed the couple to plant and grind for food only one grain of millet per day. But Abuk defied Nhialic, fearing that humanity would starve to death even before it came into being. She planted a whole field of millet, using a very long hoe. Unfortunately, she accidentally struck Nhialic with the hoe as she swung it up and down, hitting the ground and planting more millet. Nhialic did not take kindly to what he regarded as an assault by a woman who was defying his orders. How dare she? He cut the rope that connected Heaven and Earth, and

Heaven drifted far away from humanity. Thus, Nhialic withdrew from the affairs of men and women. However, Abuk was honoured for saving humanity from famine. She became a Divinity in her own right, the Mother-God of Women and Gardens.

Em-Pee bursts out laughing. Stories of her religion are much more fun than the grim ones of his. His uM-velingqangi is a distant God too, never prayed to directly but through the intercession of ancestors – those who once tasted the life of the living. Jieng's stories are also more joyful than those of the White man's religion. But what he observes in common is that it is always the defiant woman who causes the troubles of the world.

Acol bursts out laughing and adds that it is that very defiance that has made humanity possible. 'Where would the White people be if their Eva had not eaten the fruit?'

Even this laughter does not attract the jailer's attention, thanks to Slaw's high jinks. Acol still does not notice. She is steeped in the world of Divinities. Sometimes she is Acol Aretret, the unruly Acol. The Acol who wants to wreak havoc and visit her jok on everybody, including Maria-Magdalena and Monsieur Duval, and let her jok smite them to death immediately. Sometimes she is Acol Adheng, the gentle Acol. The Acol who will bide her time and let the jok plan a careful revenge. The dignified Acol.

'You are Acol Adheng today,' says Em-Pee. 'You are calm and serene.'

'You cannot trust the outward look. It will take a battle to be truly Acol Adheng. My owner is a very bad man. It will take a lot of strength to finally defeat him.'

'A man who cages a woman of such grace,' says Em-Pee. 'Not to say that those of less grace should be caged, of course.'

'Not only because of the cage. For more things. It will take dignity to defeat him. That is why I must try very hard to be Acol Adheng all the time instead of Acol Aretret.'

She is searching for her dheeng, her dignity, so that she can be truly Acol Adheng, the Acol who is filled with pride and dignity. Only then will she have enough beauty, honour, charm, elegance, nobility, grace and kindness to effect a meaningful revenge. Only then will she sing and dance. Dignity has its own aesthetic. But first she must find it.

They both turn their heads at once, attracted by Maria--Magdalena's screech. She is panicking. She comes running, waving a timepiece on a chain, with Slaw foolishly following. She chimes, 'Dinkie the Dinka, time for cards!'

Acol freezes at once.

'You know she hates that name,' says Em-Pee.

'Master and his friends will be playing cards tonight,' says Maria-Magdalena breathlessly as soon as she gets

163

to their bench. 'He'll be mad if Acol is not there. You need to get ready, Acol.'

It is not lost on Em-Pee that Acol is mad that Maria-Magdalena should mention cards. Maria-Magdalena seems ashamed that she mentioned them at all.

'You play cards then?' asks Em-Pee.

She does not respond to that question. Instead she stands up abruptly and makes to leave. Maybe she is a card player? Or maybe she photographs card players?

Maria-Magdalena gently holds her hand and says, 'Let's go, child.'

They walk a few steps, but Acol returns to him, where he is standing dumbstruck with Slaw as if trying to recover from a whirlwind.

'My mother didn't let me forget,' says Acol softly to Em-Pee, as if this is a secret. 'Even as we languished in our cage, I would forget and smile at something father said. Mother would shake her head in sorrow and say, "What Jieng man would want to marry a girl with a mouth full of teeth?"'

Acol places both her hands on her mouth, as if to make doubly sure that Em-Pee never ever sees them again.

'I would,' says Em-Pee. 'Even now I can. I want to.'

'You're not Jieng.'

'No, I am not. But I love you, teeth and all.'

'I forbid you to love me. Those I love back die. That's why I cannot love Maria-Magdalena. Those I hate live. That's why I must find other ways of destroying my owner.'

At this, she walks away. Slaw holds him back as he struggles to run after her. So he yells 'You provoked me when I had long forgotten about you. You must love me. I'm going to die in any case. We all will. You can't buy my immortality by not loving me.'

9

New York City – September 1890
The Wild Zulu

The milkman delivers a pint once a week. It used to be a pint every weekday when Aoife and Mavo were still with him, and a quart on some Fridays. He leaves it in the sun on the interior windowsill for three days until it ferments and curdles into sour milk curds. To Aoife it was spoilt when it was like that, but to Em-Pee it was a delicacy called amasi. It took him back to kwaZulu, and he enjoys it with hominy or grits overcooked into a thick paste, a poor substitute for uphuthu. But it serves the purpose.

He is enjoying this delight when an excited Slaw arrives with a packet wrapped in newsprint. 'I have something better for you to eat than your yogurt,' he says, ceremoniously unwrapping the packet.

It is a chunk of meat. Prime steak, raw. He looks at Em-Pee, expecting a comment. Or a question. Em-Pee is studying him, trying to figure out what this is all about. Slaw chants a few gibberish incantations, and breaks off a piece oozing blood. It breaks with ease. He tosses it into his mouth and chews with relish.

'Melts like butter,' he says. 'Try it.'

'No, thank you. I am not The Wild Zulu,' says Em-Pee.

'That's the thing. I have discovered the trick that makes it possible for The Wild Zulu to eat all that raw meat, and we cannot let it go to waste.'

'Cooked meat that looks raw.'

'Exactly.'

'How do you do it?'

'It's a secret.'

He will patent his invention, he says. In the meantime, there is work to be done. Dance has failed, and everyone has gone broke. Americans have decided that Zulus cannot be friendly, period. No use pursuing an ideal into which audiences are not buying. Broadway is not working out either; Davis disappeared more than eighteen months ago, after he and Em-Pee could not agree on an acceptable story. This meat will solve all their woes. They must return to the basics. They must create their own version of The Wild Zulu, pulsating with ferocity, dripping with the blood of dead animals as he eats them raw. Only it will be Slaw's specially prepared steak, and no one will be the wiser.

'I am not going to do that,' says Em-Pee.

'We'll add pepper and all the condiments you like. Don't be such a damper, man.'

'Zulus don't eat raw meat,' says Em-Pee firmly.

'We're only play-play Zulus, man. Just for fun. Just for the money. Just like Broadway.'

Slaw cannot move Em-Pee to his perspective, and this frustrates him. He gets agitated and utters a slew of accusations. Everybody sacrificed after leaving The Great Farini but Em-Pee was the one who continued to place obstacles in their way. The troupe would have made it big if it were not for him. They left The Great Farini because of him – at this Em-Pee grunts his surprise – but right from the beginning he shot down every great idea that would have made them rich. They endured still and stayed with him through all the seven years. All that time he showed how ungrateful he was. He was so proud that he even turned down a Broadway offer, offending Davis, a great impresario who would have changed their fortunes. Even when Davis wanted to put his own money down to purchase Dinkie the Dinka Princess from Duval, Em-Pee stood against that. And now of course Davis is gone. Most likely they will never see him again.

Slaw adds that he is no longer prepared to tolerate Em-Pee's nonsense. He will not die a pauper in America. He is proceeding with all the projects that Em-Pee turned down. He is going to get his own Zulus who will eat his raw meat. He is marrying Maria-Magdalena and will take over Dinkie the Dinka Princess. He is going to be the greatest impresario of all time, and Em-Pee cannot stop him. He is sick and tired of ambitionless

Negroes. With or without them, he is going to be greater than The Great Farini. He is going to be greater than P.T. Barnum. He is going to be greater than J.A. Bailey.

Em-Pee is unmoved throughout this diatribe. Until Slaw mentions Dinkie the Dinka Princess. At this, his ears prick up.

'You are not!' he says.

'Wait and see and worship in my shadow.'

'You're not taking over Dinkie ... Acol.'

'I am too. Me and Maria-Magdalena, we're engaged to be married.'

'But you are not getting anywhere near Acol.'

'If I can raise enough money for Duval, yes I am.'

Em-Pee pounces on Slaw. He presses his head against the wall but stops his fist midway before it connects with his jaw. Instead he reaches for the meat and rubs it in his face. Then he dashes out the door, leaving a heaving and cringing Slaw on the floor of his tenement.

He runs all the way to Madison Avenue, ignoring the stares and the hollers, not even considering the likelihood that he may be mistaken for a thief and have a throng of do-gooders chasing him. Fortunately, New Yorkers manage to mind their own business for a change.

He knocks at Duval's door. Banging with both hands, and then with the clown-faced knocker. He does not care if Duval is at home or not. On the previous occasions he always made certain the master was away before he knocked. He has seen Duval only from a distance. A week ago Duval almost caught Em-Pee talking to Acol on the steps – one of the few occasions in the past one year he has visited Acol and had a coherent conversation with her.

As he bangs on the door, waiting a moment or two and then banging again, he recalls how on each occasion he came and Maria-Magdalena arranged a meeting at the park, or in the kitchen if no other servant was present, he would ask, 'Which Acol are you today?' If she said Acol Aretret he knew immediately they would not get along. She was the unruly Acol, the Acol whose mind was full of nothing but murder, the Acol preoccupied only with cajoling her jok to hasten her revenge. He would have to return on another day. Not even Maria-Magdalena could manage Acol Aretret.

The day Duval almost caught them together she was Acol Adheng, the gentle Acol, and was ready to spend the afternoon with him in the park. Perhaps she was Acol Adheng because she had not been displayed in the cage that morning.

She and Em-Pee were talking outside the house, trying to decide whether or not she should take the camera, promising that maybe today she would finally take his photo after all these years. And then Duval's carriage arrived. She saw it from a distance and scurried up the steps into the house without so much as a goodbye.

He bangs at the door again. And waits. Finally, he hears shuffling footsteps. The door swings open and Maria-Magdalena, in a mud facial and a heavy dressing gown, though it's afternoon already, glares at him.

'You and Slaw ...' Em-Pee begins.

'The master is here today,' she whispers.

'I don't care,' he yells. 'I want him out here too. I want him to hear of your treachery. You and Slaw are in some kind of courtship?'

'Yes, we are getting married. Do we need your permission for that?'

'None of you are going to touch Acol. Do you hear that? None of you!'

'Why would we want to touch Acol?'

He will not get anywhere with this smug woman. He leaves her standing at the door, arms folded on her chest.

At first he has no idea where to go. He feels helpless. He must find a way to save Acol. Not just save her, but have her as his own. He cannot buy her from Duval. He has no money to do so. He does not even know that he would find it in himself to purchase her if he had the money. He cannot even suggest that they elope to some faraway state where the bourbon-soaked owner would not find them. No one has the right to own anyone anyway. Slavery was long abolished, though it still exists, as Acol's case clearly shows. But he knows she would not agree to eloping. She is preoccupied with her jok, who must mete out vengeance. And her jok is biding her time. In any event, he would not have the money to elope with her even if she were to agree. Money. It is the problem. It is also the solution.

Skildore Skolnik! The producer at Niblo's. He can go cap in hand and beg for the Cetshwayo Project to be resuscitated. He has grown, and now understands that he cannot starve for authenticity. He will tell him that he is willing to have as many devils and demons in the play as Skolnik likes. As long as he puts some money down, takes on the project, and produces *Battle of Isandlwana* at Niblo's on Broadway. He can bring in his Ulundi Christian victory over heathens, for all he cares. Skildore is a sharp businessman. Surely he will seize the opportunity.

The only damper would be if Skildore is no longer at Niblo's. After all, it's been three years.

Skildore Skolnik is there all right, and is as sourpuss as ever. He berates Em-Pee, without giving him the opportunity to respond. At first, Em-Pee thinks it is for his resistance to demons and devils, and tries to get a word in edgeways that these days he loves the idea of a king possessed by demons and devils and wants to get on with the project even without Davis, but he discovers that Skolnik's anger has something to do with having been robbed by the same Davis. Apparently, he had been seeing Davis, without Em-Pee, and had finally reached an agreement on the story. Davis, however, requested an advance of some considerable amount so that he could focus on polishing the story according to Skolnik's specifications. He had fallen on challenging times, he said, since neglecting his work as an impresario because of this play. An agreement was signed and Skolnik parted with the funds. And parted with Davis. He has not seen him since.

'I'll find Davis,' says Em-Pee. 'I will bring him back here. We still want to do the play.'

'Not with Niblo's, I am afraid.'

He has an inkling of where Davis lives. He recalls the walks with him from his Mulberry Street tenement to the rows of brownstone mansions of upper-crust Manhattanites near the Madison Square Park area, where Davis hurried into one of them. He may be able to identify it.

Davis's mansion is more imposing than Duval's. He is directed to the service entrance and pleads with the manservant, saying that he would like to see the master of the house about an urgent matter that is to the master's benefit. He is led into the presence of a gigantic Mulatto man wearing boxing shorts and a flowing silk bathrobe. He is sitting at a mammoth walnut desk doing some paperwork.

'He says he has something important to tell you, sir,' says the manservant.

The Mulatto man peers at Em-Pee curiously and beckons him to approach his desk. He looks vaguely familiar.

'Not you, sir. Mr Davis. It is Mr Davis I want,' stammers Em-Pee.

'You said the master of the house,' says the manservant.

The man signals the manservant to leave and asks Em-Pee to take a seat. He tries to display a friendly mien, which still cannot but be unsettling. Perhaps he is aware of this because he stretches his hand out, grabs Em-Pee's firmly, and introduces himself as Mr Dominic Alef.

'From Africa?' he asks.

Em-Pee nods.

'How does our Davis know a brother from Africa?'

Em-Pee tells him about the project they are working on together.

'Niblo's? That's Broadway,' booms Alef. 'That's big time. And how did you know Davis in the first place … to be working with him on Broadway?'

He tells him about The Wild Zulu. How Davis arranged for him to see one of the shows he curated so that he may learn a few tricks for his own troupe that had just broken away from The Great Farini.

'You know important people, my friend,' says Alef, shaking his head as if he pities Em-Pee for it. 'You know The Great Farini. And, guess what, now you know The Wild Zulu.'

He is The Wild Zulu. A lighter version. The version before it browns itself with boot polish. Or with whatever it is Whites and Mulattoes use to tan themselves into Zulus. And he is amused at Em-Pee's wide-eyed awe. He bursts out laughing, and hollers to his servants that they should bring Davis before him forthwith.

Dominic Alef owns himself as The Wild Zulu. He is his own impresario and owns Davis, who is only the White front of the business. The pretend-impresario the White business world will be comfortable dealing with. Originally a carnival strongman from New Orleans, Alef came to New York as an indigent at the height of the Zulu craze, established himself as a savage, and is now minting it, living a regal life in a big house full of mostly White servants.

Davis drags himself into Alef's study. He is nothing like the self-assured and brash Davis he last saw. Em-Pee is not sure if he is intoxicated. He looks groggy. And bruised. He starts a bit when he sees Em-Pee, but soon composes himself.

'Know him?' asks Alef.

'Never seen him,' says Davis, shaking his head.

'You stole my secrets for him, to make him a better Zulu than me,' says Alef calmly. But he is not fooling anyone, least of all Davis; it is the calm before the storm. And it is a storm he knows too well.

'What other secret did you sell him? The meat? That

the parts I eat are not really raw? That I don't really eat the chicken but rip it open with sharp artificial metal nails to spray the blood all over and I only chew the feathers?'

'No, not the meat! Not the chicken!' says Davis, beginning to back away from him. But the big man beckons him, and he timidly returns.

Alef gives him a few whacks on the face with an open hand. Before fists can rain on him, he is squirming on the ground.

By the time Em-Pee leaves Alef's mansion he knows the source of Davis's accident proneness. He is aware that Davis continued to meet Slaw secretly and is part of the conspiracy to purchase Dinkie the Dinka Princess. The deal has not gone through yet, only because of a lack of funds. He knows that Slaw's discovery of how to tenderise meat and cook it while it remains red as if raw, was in fact stolen by Davis from Alef. Davis has been trying to work his way out of this bondage for years, stealing ideas and cash, hoping to be an independent impresario in his own right one day. He knows that the money from Niblo's has aggravated his bondage; Alef wants every cent of it for himself. Alef says it rightly belongs to him, as Davis had no right to make deals on his own. Davis must find a way of paying it back, not to Skolnik, but to Alef.

As he walks out of the back gate, Em-Pee wonders

what Davis meant when he accused him of selling him
out to Alef for a woman who is nothing but a cards-
whore. What on earth is a cards-whore?

10

New York City – October 1892
The Passing Carnival

This is how it begins. The passing carnival. He steps out of the tenement all spruced up and walks down the squeaky steps. The first human of the day is Millie, the Negro matron who teaches elementary school at Baxter Street. He finds her interesting and at one time thought they could date. She liked him. She initiated the liking and exhibited it with coy smiles and winks. But soon he realised she didn't want to be seen with him in public. On one occasion they went out to dinner, and on another to an Irish pub. On both occasions, whenever good-looking, well-heeled Coloured folk entered, she turned her back on him, pretending she was on her own, and that the man just happened to be sitting close to her by chance. He decided that if Millie didn't want to be seen with him, then she won't be seen with him. When he ignored her, she felt insulted and rubbished him in the neighbourhood. Who does he think he is, a dancing jungle bunny from Africa getting all haughty in the city of New York?

That was before Acol. Before she existed in the flesh and then became a memory. She has been a memory for months already. A memory of the flesh, because the process and the product of recollection act upon Em-Pee in visible ways. That's what memories do in a world that involves Acol. They do not live only in the mind and end their existence there; they are projected as images that have an external presence in the present. They act from the inside to the outside of the one who remembers, eating him alive, lashing him till he bleeds. Or caressing his body, creating pleasant sensations, evoking tingling joy. It is the way of the Jieng that he learned from her, while at the same time forcing her body to learn how to remember. Memory acts on you in the same manner the source of that memory did. Acol disappeared months ago, but her memory continues to make demands on him. It continues to confer benefits on him too. Flights of euphoria.

The passing carnival may keep Acol at bay for a while today. An essential distraction. How strong it will be, Em-Pee has no idea. Yesterday could have signalled that he should find a distraction much more enduring than a passing carnival. He was drifting around the brownstone mansions as he is wont to do whenever memory assails him. Confronted by the silence that has become a visible feature of Monsieur Duval's home. Until yesterday, when the silence was broken. Wagon after wagon loading furniture from the house and transporting it to auction houses. Em-Pee lends a hand, for it brings him closer to the action and the gossip. Workmen hammering up signs that the mansion itself will be auctioned on a specific date. Folks gathering to watch, for the demise of one neighbour is entertainment for another. Neighbours, mostly the servitude class, wondering what could have happened. Duval had gone insane. The previous night he grabbed his shimmering Remington Model 1890 revolver and blew his head off. Em-Pee wonders if this could be the long-awaited jok's revenge. But how does the jok avenge her ward in her absence? How does the jok establish her own regime in the absence of the body over which she is guardian? Where is the jok's ward?

The neighbours do not hear these questions, for they are in Em-Pee's head. But the neighbours answer them still: they say the man sent the Black girl to a mental asylum in the state of Ohio. In a small college town called Athens. There she is confined, and most likely there her grave will be. World without end. Amen.

Carnivals are another way of remembering.

Millie is at the window. She seems to spend a lot of time at the window the older a maid she becomes. He waves and blows her a kiss. They have learned to live with each other. Each in her or his prescribed box. She steps out and offers him a mug of coffee if he's not in too much of a hurry. They stand at the door while he drinks the coffee. They complain how no one wants to do anything to clean up the rookery.

The passing carnival is on the Bowery. He was not invited. He is not one of the revellers. Not one of the official revellers, that is. But he will revel all the same. When Samson told him about it, he decided to attend. He is a veteran too, whether The Great Farini likes it or not. He may not march with the other stars of the carnival, or sit on a flower-bedecked wagon, but he was part of the history-making epoch and will be there. They will see him, all dressed up impeccably, an elegant New Yorker in a well-tailored tweed suit, brown like his skin, custom-made, and a brown bowler hat, not a cap – a bowler hat like the gentleman he is.

A brass band leads, and everyone else follows. The Great Farini is celebrating his veterans. Stars who have attracted spectators over the years, some of whom have had such longevity that they are still drawcards. And many others who live only in memory. He wonders if he will see his old mates among the honoured, those who returned to Farini after the Genu-Wine Zulus and all its incarnations crashed, but also those Farini sold to other acts but continue to be on good terms with him.

Em-Pee has kept contact with Samson, only because he has continued to live at the old Mulberry Street bordello where he has been a useful point man for some of his colleagues in need of carnal relief.

He casts his eyes on the floats, and on the marchers, and wonders if Slaw will be anywhere in sight. The last time he saw him was when he left him squirming in his tenement, after the incident with the meat. When Em-Pee returned, Slaw had trashed his tenement and left.

A man is waving. Em-Pee looks around to make sure it is for him the wave is meant. He waves back. The big smile and big teeth that fill the mouth tell him at once that it is Mkano, known by one and all as Zulu Charley. He never worked with him but made his acquaintance when he was part of the exhibit at Bunnell's Museum on Broadway and 9th Street. One thing that distinguished him from most of the Zulus he knew was that Zulu Charley was a genuine Zulu from the occupied territory of Natal. Em-Pee used to relish speaking isiZulu with him, to the mystification of all the other Zulus and sundry spectators at the museum.

Zulu Charley waves frenziedly, laughing his cares away. Em-Pee waves back, also returning the laughter. His chortles get louder when he remembers how irrepressible Zulu Charley used to be. He also remembers an incident one December ten years ago when Mkano was in the news for assaulting an actor with a three-foot pole. Apparently the actor had called him all sorts of insulting names, and even raised his hand to him. That was when Mkano flipped his lid and hit the man. Everyone thought he would be locked up for a long time. As a

Negro, you didn't hit a White man and get away with it. But many witnesses spoke of Zulu Charley's patience, how he tried to ignore the actor's taunts, and even walked away to another part of the room; how the bully followed him and continued with his insolence, and how Mkano lost it only when the actor raised his hand to him.

People didn't toy with Zulu Charley after that.

As Em-Pee marches on the sidelines, watching Zulu Charley's wave that has now turned into a dance, he wonders what could have happened to Anita, Zulu Charley's wife. Everything about Zulu Charley was sensational. So was his marriage to Anita, an Italian girl he met when she came to watch the re-enactment of the Battle of Rorke's Drift, another Anglo-Zulu engagement that was popular because the British Red Coats were able to defend a fort against a Zulu force much superior in numbers. The Italian girl was attracted to the Zulu warrior. Their engagement caused some sensation, with Anita's parents threatening to disown her. Newspapers wrote of this romance in terms of a Shakespearean tragedy, Zulu Charley being Othello, Anita Desdemona and her father Brabantio. The last time Em-Pee heard of the couple, their marriage had had its ups and downs, with Anita leaving him at one point, and then rumoured to have returned it was much like the highs and lows of his own union with Aoife, although his was never in the papers, and the final low never became a high again.

Em-Pee recognises the horsemen as well. They are the American Indians who raced with the Zulus at some of the events. And there is the two-headed woman on one of the floats. He remembers her as two women. Conjoined twins, dressed to appear as one person. They are chit-chatting with another woman. Princess Amadaga! Farini's sensational surprise of the eighties at the height of King Cetshwayo's fame. Princess Amadaga, Cetshwayo's own daughter. Em-Pee remembers how graceful she was when she was first introduced at Bunnell's, and how the audiences went berserk, pushing and shoving just to get a glimpse of her. This was one of The Great Farini's greatest coups. And now here she is, sitting on a flower-bedecked wagon with divers human oddities.

Em-Pee waves at Princess Amadaga. She does not wave back. Perhaps she does not remember him. They met only once, when Em-Pee felt it would be remiss if he did not pay his respects to the daughter of his king. He didn't expect to recognise her; the king had many daughters from many different wives. But he was hoping that, in their conversation, they would have some people in common. Maybe even Nomalanga. The princess might know what had finally happened to her, the torrid woman who sparked his escape from the kingdom.

After negotiating and bribing his way to the back rooms of the museum where exhibits and performers awaited their turn to appear on stage, he was finally in the presence of the princess. She was sitting on a wooden crate, trying to sing a Mulatto baby in her arms to sleep. He could not understand the words, but they were in a language with which he was not familiar. No one had mentioned that Princess Amadaga had a baby.

'Sawubona we Nkosazana!' he greeted in isiZulu, bowing before her. 'We see you, Your Royal Highness!'

She seemed mystified. She obviously did not understand what he was saying.

She was brown. But it was the brownness of the islands.

He did not understand why he was disappointed as he left the museum. After all, everyone is an African prince or princess when they come to America. He himself was once a prince too, but in England. He gave up the title after he came to America and found the country overrun with African royalty of all sizes, shapes and hues.

* * *

The passing carnival takes him across Brooklyn Bridge. It is no longer Farini's. It's only Em-Pee and some brethren he was introduced to by Mkano at one of the stations. The carriage that carries them belongs to missionaries and proclaims that fact in bold red and white paint on its exterior. The brethren speak isiZulu in cadences that should variously be echoed by the deep uKhahlamba

Mountains, the Valley of a Thousand Hills where the uMngeni and uMsunduzi rivers meet, and the white sands of the southern coast.

The one whose opinion they seem to listen to is older and has a gentle tone but gets excitable when he narrates events of import to himself or the others. His face is smooth and unfurrowed by memory, in contrast to Em-Pee's own, which is marred by gullies of remembering. The man is yet to build storage places of memory in his body. The lumps and knots that Em-Pee can feel in his own body have not accumulated in any of these brethren.

They are students from amakholwa families, the Christian converts of kwaZulu, newly arrived in America, hence the tour of New York City. The tour guide is Freddy Coomerlow, a graduate of the Hampton Institute, Virginia, where he specialised in blacksmithing and wheelwrighting. The fresh-faced brethren are en route to the same institution, some to study the same subjects, others carpentry and agriculture.

Coomerlow is entertaining them with stories of faux-Zulus in New York, a phenomenon that amazes them, angers some and bewilders others. All disguise their true feelings with incredulous chuckles. Em-Pee squirms; he is part of the industry they are discussing, though he doubts if any one of them knows that. Unless Coomerlow took note when Mkano introduced him as a former colleague.

'It is true,' says Coomerlow, as if they are questioning his integrity. 'I have encountered enough fake Zulus in the streets of New York to last me a lifetime.'

From his leather train case he takes out an old copy of *Atlantic Monthly* and reads aloud for them: *The idea that the Dimes Museum Zulus are manufactured to order is false. There have been Zulus. These are not, as some of the journalists have wickedly insinuated, Irish immigrants cunningly painted and made up like savages. They are genuine Zulus; and though we need not believe the lecturer's statement that they fought under Cetewayo at Isandhwayo, and displayed prodigies of valor in order to free their country from British rule, there is no doubt that they would prove terrible enemies in battle.*

'Guess what?' says Coomerlow after his dramatic reading. 'They were indeed Irish immigrants painted brown!'

The laughter only stops when the passing carnival arrives at the home of John Langalibalele Dube in Brooklyn. He is introduced to Em-Pee and the students as a man of letters, a newspaper editor and publisher. He is the one who has arranged for these students, through the Congregationalist American Board of Commissioners for Foreign Missions, to come to America to study.

'Surely, you are a little bit too mature to be one of the students,' says Dube, looking at Em-Pee benevolently.

'He is a mfowethu from Ondini we met at a carnival

in Manhattan,' says Coomerlow. 'He said he was free, so I invited him to meet his brothers from home.'

As they sit at the meal of uphuthu made of very rough corn meal, meat and vegetables, Dube regales them with his experiences in America where he has lived for three years, some of which were spent at Oberlin College in Ohio. This is his final year and he is looking forward to returning home, where there is a lot of work to be done.

After hearing Em-Pee's story, that he came as a dancer via England, the men encourage him to also try to find his way home, because there is work to be done.

Coomerlow is sceptical, though. 'The man is paid in America to dance. At home you cannot eat the dance,' he says.

'The man can learn a trade. He can learn agriculture and return home to work for the self-sufficiency of his people,' says Dube.

'Or he can go to Oberlin College and then to the Chicago Medical College and become a doctor like Nembula,' says Coomerlow testily.

Dube is irritated, but for the sake of the visitors he controls himself. Obviously Coomerlow is challenging him, and this must be an ongoing debate that neither Em-Pee nor the students know anything about.

'You talk as if I don't want amaZulu to be doctors. I arranged for Dr Nembula to come here and study medicine.'

It is a question of focus, Coomerlow says. Though he has benefited from industrial training, he objects to the fact that the American missionaries are focusing on that to the exclusion of liberal education – what he calls book education. Dube argues that training in the trades is what amaZulu need at this point for self-sufficiency from the oppressive system of White domination. That is why he is working very hard to establish trade schools in his country, patterned along the Hampton-Tuskegee model.

'I do not see the self-sufficiency, sir,' says Coomerlow.

He does not believe the training he received will give him freedom from the White man once he returns home. He has been trained for a subordinate role, to serve the White man more efficiently.

'So, in your mind, Freddy, we'll be slaves forever? All these efforts to fight for freedom will come to naught?'

'What good is trade training going to do for everyone else?' asks Coomerlow. 'I know it's going to make me a good worker for the White man who owns the wagon factory. But is it going to make *me* own the wagon factory?'

'The law won't allow you to own it now. But when we are free you'll own it,' pipes up one of the students.

Dube smiles approvingly, looking at Coomerlow and shaking his head as if to say 'look at you, even a greenhorn student sees the light better than you do'.

'Maybe they should send you to Oberlin, Ohio, where you'll learn things that are above your station in life, so that you can use your brains on books instead of using your hands on hammering wrought iron into shape.' Coomerlow is addressing the student. No one is sure whether or not he is being sarcastic.

Em-Pee detects some acrimony that has spoiled the erstwhile gentle tone. He is sorry that his dancing started this debate. These are issues he will think about one day. Not now. The mention of Ohio has left him unsettled.

In Ohio a jok lives, guarding a purple-coloured woman in a mental asylum.

11

Athens, Ohio – May 1893
Searching for the Atoc Bird

Psychiatrists, from the time the word was coined by Professor Johann Christian Reil in 1808, if not from earlier, have been at odds with the gods. They reduce prophetic voices to faulty perceptions and dismiss divine flight as withdrawal from reality. The age-old battle continues in Acol's ward at the Athens Lunatic Asylum. She says it is her jok, a personal divinity gone unruly; they say it is syphilis gone to her head.

They let her roam the woods, a privilege they do not grant any of the other female inmates, who are here for a variety of maladies ranging from melancholia to such forms of madness as irregular menstruation, uterus problems and female hysteria – women whose madness is womanhood.

She is not from here; the only place she can escape to is here. She is at home here. She thinks of no other home. Wishes for no other home. Is at peace with herself and her life. As long as she can wander in the woods searching for things to photograph, and as long as the rolls of film and emulsion that Maria-Magdalena made certain she packed in her boxes last. Thanks to an anonymous benefactor, who Acol suspects is the same Maria-Magdalena, she has since upgraded from the ancient Scovill to the new Kodak camera first introduced five years ago.

They give her the leeway with pleasure, including the use of a broom closet as a darkroom. It benefits them to have a resident photographer among the inmates. When they catch her in a good mood, she even agrees to photograph their babies and their pets.

Em-Pee discovers her sitting at the pond, drawing invisible pictures on the water with her finger. She breaks into a smile immediately she sees him. Tranquillity shines in her eyes.

'Who are you today?' Em-Pee asks. 'Don't tell me. You are Acol Adheng.'

'How do you know?' she asks, smiling and nodding in the affirmative.

'Your owner is dead,' says Em-Pee, ignoring her question. 'Shot himself.'

She does not look surprised at all. It is as if she knows already.

'No, he did not.'

'I went there and talked with the neighbours. They say he shot himself with a brand-new gun which he bought especially for that purpose.'

'My hand did it,' she says, waving her hand dismissively.

'You were already here when it happened,' says Em-Pee cautiously, not wanting to agitate her by seeming to suggest she is a liar. 'Weren't you?'

'It's my hand that held the Remington, not his,' she says indifferently. 'He screamed for mercy. Just as I screamed when they did all those things to me. But there was no one to hear him. Maria-Magdalena was gallivanting with her Slaw. It was just me and him. And my hand had no mercy in it. He screamed, and my hand pulled the trigger.'

'You did?' he asks incredulously. 'And you even know it was a Remington!'

'My hand did.'

He smiles as clarity dawns on him. 'Your jok's hand?'

'The Divinities were taking their time. I had become too impatient. I did it myself with my own hand. Of course, my jok guided it.'

'It was your jok!'

'You cannot separate the two,' she says. 'Anyway, it changes nothing. It is divine retaliation on me, not him. He is no longer here to feel the punishment; I am.'

She does not want to talk about this any more. She wants to talk about happy things instead. She demands he tell her only happy things.

'I am on my way to Chicago,' he says.

193

'How is that a happy thing?'

It is a happy thing because it is the only way he will be able to return to Africa. And he needs to return; the urge is even greater now that he met his countrymen who are doing remarkable things in America and are all working towards returning home to do similar great things there. He tells her about Dr Nembula, who he did not meet but about whose work he heard wonderful things, not only as a medical doctor but as an activist in cooperative agriculture and other community upliftment projects; about Langalibalele Dube, a great man of learning, also tirelessly working for progress and the emancipation of the entire Black race, not just amaZulu; the students who have come to acquire skills that will make them just as good as White people in kwaZulu; and Freddy Coomerlow, a very intelligent rebel who may not return home but is likely to stay here and accumulate wealth as a wheelwright. At least, that's what his argument indicated to Em-Pee: disillusionment with the situation in the old country.

'These men don't dance for the White man,' says Em-Pee.

He has stopped dancing. But only until he gets home. When he gets home, he will dance for his people. And with them. For everyone in his homeland is a dancer.

Dance is a way of life. It is a way of death too. It is a way of healing, of ancestral veneration, of praying, of working, of making love, of eating and drinking. It is a way of celebration, though he has little to celebrate. He has a long way to go before he catches up with his age-mates. As he struggled to make it in America as an independent performer, his mates back home were making strides in the society, accumulating wealth, marrying wives, ploughing fields, owning cattle, participating in the affairs of the state, and gaining respect and prestige.

He is returning with nothing; his only wealth is his son, Mavo. Where he came from he was a statesman, part of the military and chief class, so close to the king that he bathed him.

But here in the land of the White man he is just a performing monkey.

Now, he is going to sell his labour in Chicago, where he heard there is a demand for authentic Zulus. Not to dance, but to work.

The 1893 World's Columbian Exposition opened on 1 May and will run until 30 October. It is the biggest international trade fair ever organised on American soil and celebrates the four-hundredth anniversary of the discovery of the New World by Christopher Columbus. There are exhibits from many countries and cultures, including Africans from Togo and Dahomey on display in all their 'primitive' splendour, to contrast them with the glittering achievements of American civilisation. From the Cape Colony there are ostrich, wool and mohair products on display.

The biggest attraction, apart from the Viking ship built in Norway to specifications based on a model discovered near Sandefjord that had sailed from that country through the Great Lakes to Chicago, is the replica of a Kimberley diamond mine constructed by De Beers Diamond Corporation. It is more than two thousand feet tall. The company also shipped to Chicago, all the way from southern Africa, thousands of bags of original earth from the rich Kimberley diamond fields to be spread in the exhibit area, in which real diamonds worth more than a million dollars are seeded.

That's where the Zulus come in. They have been employed to guard the diamonds and can be seen prancing about in their skins and feather costumes, armed with shields and assegais. Besides acting as security guards, they also run the machine that washes the diamonds before they are polished and cut by lapidaries from Tiffany and Company.

These are authentic Zulus who came on a ship to work at this international fair and will be sailing back home in November. Em-Pee is on his way to join them. He hopes to secure employment with the company and return with them to the Cape Colony at the end of the fair.

'I want to return with you and Mavo,' says Em-Pee.

But Acol is not there. He was so engrossed in telling

his tale he did not see her leave. He does not even know when she left. He might have been talking to himself all this time.

'Acol!'

He hears breaking twigs and walks in that direction. There she is, tiptoeing between the trees, camera at the ready as if it is a lethal weapon and she is a hunter. When she spots him she shushes him, creeps behind a tree, and then gives up in frustration.

'You scared it away!' she says. 'I'm mad at you.'

It is a beautiful way of being mad at him because she does not look mad at all. Not even frustrated any more. Instead she smiles, her smooth purple skin reflecting the glow of light that sneaks in between the trees.

She is looking for the atoc bird, she says. It is quite elusive, but she has the patience. She has her whole life before her to look for the atoc.

'How will you know when you find the atoc? How is it different from other birds?'

'Atoc is a bird of my childhood.'

She describes it with so much affection, shaping her hands to show its size, while supporting the camera with her arm against her breast. It is grey in colour, like some of the pigeons she has seen around here. She once thought one of them was an atoc. But it was not. An atoc has an orange beak and yellow cheeks. It has a snow-white chest bordered by black feathers.

The atoc, what a delightful bird!

He marvels at this. She is living proof of what she taught him: remembering externalises past experiences in the present. She is looking for an atoc, a bird of her memory. She will find the south Sudanese bird in the spring climes of Appalachian Ohio.

'I want to help you find it,' says Em-Pee.

She finds this suggestion exciting and leads him to a spot under another tree, where she has her lace dress purse hanging on a low branch. She takes out a few photographs and shows him some where she almost caught the atoc. Em-Pee can see only leaves, rocks and even headstones of graves.

But none has an atoc. He says so, and she chastises him for not being too bright.

'I told you I didn't catch the atoc. I *almost* caught it.'

She gives him one picture that she says has an atoc in it.

'There it is, sitting on a log.'

Em-Pee can see the water, and the log floating on the pond. He cannot see any atoc though, unless one wants to be generous and call a dark-grey spot on a light-grey log an atoc. He will not lie to her. He confesses that perhaps he doesn't have enough enlightenment at this point to see an atoc.

'Here it is, man, preening itself on the log.' She is getting exasperated.

Em-Pee shakes his head, no. She breaks into a smile and promises that she will not rest till she gets the perfect shot that even he can see.

'You can't even see an atoc, and yet you say you want to take me to Africa?'

'Yes, I want to go to Africa with you. You will teach me how to see atocs,' he says, grateful that she has brought up the subject. 'I will see as many atocs as you like.'

She giggles, as if she is enjoying his desperation. 'I must find an atoc.'

'I said I will help you.'

At this he takes her hand. She cringes slightly and gently tries to slide it out of his. He won't let go, but instead grabs it with both hands, pleadingly. This makes her frantic, as if she is having a panic attack. She screams that he must leave her hand alone.

He lets go and is shaken that his touch had this effect on her. He has touched her before without any drama. She has touched him too. Why, she has even touched him in hidden places.

'I must honour the memory of the harm inflicted on me,' she says, walking away from him. She wants to go back to her ward.

He will not let this go. He wants to know what it all means.

Could this be the memory of the cage that must be honoured?

'It is more than the cage. Much more,' she says. 'Maria-Magdalena must have told you. She said she would when she was trying to force me to stop seeing you.'

It is all about the cards. The cards always make her shudder.

The owner was a gambler and played them every weekend. When his fortunes plummeted, he played them on some weekdays as well — every day, some weeks. And she had to be there for every game. Even as she walks in the tranquil grounds of the Athens Lunatic Asylum, she can hear Maria-Magdalena's voice ringing like a bell, 'Dinkie the Dinka, time for cards!'

When she hears that call, she gets confused. She must run to the pond, where it never reaches. She must look for the atoc in the water, on the grass, on the floating logs, on the leaves, until the ringing call has receded to silence in her head.

It started as a joke when Monsieur Duval's poker mates had gathered around the table, and the owner was on a losing streak. He had what he thought was a good hand to recoup his losses but had nothing to put in the pot. So he put in Dinkie the Dinka Princess.

She was commanded to march to a guest room upstairs where the winner would have his way with her. She fought and kicked and bit the manservants who dragged her up the spiral staircase. She screamed to Maria-Magdalena to save her but she sat motionlessly in the kitchen, shutting out the screams with her own humming of a nursery jingle.

Dinkie the Dinka Princess was repeatedly raped by the owner and sundry winners, who came in all shapes and sizes. Every time it happened she fought and scratched, even biting them with her teeth. That's when she realised that bottom teeth, though so ayur – so undignified and shameful – can be a force for good.

She was bruised and exhausted after each card game. But she also exhausted winners who would have their way only after a struggle.

Soon they threatened to opt for money or property instead of her as a prize. That's when the chaining began. Even as the game was going on, she would already be chained to the bed frame. It did not matter how many hours the game took, she had to lie there and wait. Sometimes only in the early hours of the morning would the winner enter the room and have his way with her. She fought still, despite being in chains. And lost. Always.

Later she realised that her fierce fighting aroused some of them and made them enjoy her even more. She deprived them of that pleasure by lying still on the bed as they injected their death into her.

Em-Pee allows his tears to flow freely. Yet she is smiling the most beatific smile, making his tears drench his face and shirt even more profusely.

He will never get over the realisation that when she touched him in hidden places she was saving him from the disease.

12

Union-America Line – November 1893
She is Nhialic She is God

The heat threatens to send him running up onto the deck and then diving into the St Lawrence River. He is attending to four furnaces, feeding one with coal for about two minutes, then turning to the next. He thinks he knows how a pig feels when it is roasted on a spit. This will be the stoker's lot every day for the coming weeks, until the Union-America Line steamship docks in Cape Town.

Then he will walk free. He will no longer be beholden to anyone. It will be the end of his servitude to De Beers Diamond Corporation, which employed him at the World's Columbian Exposition and paid for his passage back home, together with the rest of the Zulus, who now spend their time singing in steerage. It will also be the end of his servitude to the Union-America Line, which allowed him to take his son aboard provided he paid for his passage by working with the stokers.

There were some problems with harbour officials in Chicago. They did not want him to take Mavo on board with him.

'The boy is almost White,' said an official. 'We cannot allow him to take an American boy with him to Africa.'

After a lot of arguing, presentation of documents, and intervention by the De Beers people, permission was granted – just when he was about to give up and return to New York with his son.

After a four-hour shift he joins Mavo in steerage. He is a brooding boy, and Em-Pee hopes he will get over his being uprooted from the only life he has known in New York for an uncertain one in the land of his father. He was excited at first, particularly about the voyage. But confinement is beginning to get to him. It will be worse in days to come.

Mavo is reading a book when Em-Pee sits next to him. Em-Pee is glad that his son has become bookish. He utters a few words of encouragement and tells him about the life he imagines awaits them in the rolling hills of kwaZulu. As soon as they touch that soil, Em-Pee will be dead and Mpiyezintombi Mkhize will be reborn.

'Where we are going, no one knows Em-Pee. They only know Mpiyezintombi. Better start practising it. You'll be lost if you call me Em-Pee.' At this he chortles, and Mavo smiles.

But the smile changes to concern when the haunted look he has occasionally seen on his father returns.

'You know, Mavovo, sometimes we need to learn that we can love from a distance and do nothing about it. We don't have to own what we love.'

Mavo goes through the motions of agreeing with his father. He is only being polite. He has no idea what he is talking about.

He is, of course, talking about Acol. It is the same thing that he told her in their final conversation at the Athens Lunatic Asylum before his departure for Chicago, when he finally gave up on her. When she remained calm and beautiful and resolute despite his begging. When she asked, 'What you want me for, how is it different from what men have always wanted me for?' and he responded, 'It is different because I love you. I never said this to any woman – not even to my wife.' And she laughed mockingly and said, 'You should have heard the beautiful things they whispered in my ear as they tore me apart, injecting death into my person.'

It is her defiance that he will always remember. She defied even God as she declared herself one. She stood there, in Em-Pee's face, and said without rancour in her voice, 'I am myself Nhialic! I am myself God! I go with no one but myself.'

Em-Pee understood completely what she meant. She would not be rescued by a man. Instead she rescued herself by externalising memories of her childhood world and re-creating it in the vast wilderness of the asylum, using the power of her Jieng spiritual realm. Thus, she has regained her freedom.

He and Mavo have regained their freedom too. Or are on a voyage towards that goal. Whether you choose to see it that way or not, it is a story with a happy ending.

Acol will always be a strong presence in her absence. Like the God she is. She taught him how to externalise memory and make its object part of the present reality. She will therefore only cease to exist when he dies. Her mortality depends on his. Those lessons will come in handy throughout this voyage and in the life ahead.

The end is always a journey.